All or
NOTHING

ALL OR NOTHING
Copyright © 2016 by Susan Roth

Cover by Kanaxa

roselerner.com

Table of Contents

For my great-grandmother Rose,
WHO GOT OUT.

Acknowledgments

This novella was originally published in the anthology *Gambled Away*. I want to thank Molly O'Keefe for being as excited as me when we had the idea on Twitter one day. I am so proud to have been part of it!

A million thanks to my insightful, generous critique partners and beta readers: Tiffany Ruzicki, Kate Addison, Greg Holt, Aleksei Valentin, L. Anthony Graham, Ariella Bouskila, Melanie Kress, Charlotte Russell, Alyssa Everett, Susanna Fraser. I love you. Any remaining mistakes and bad decisions are of course entirely mine.

Extra-special thanks to Olivia Waite for telling me it felt like I was holding something back. I was.

And as always, thanks to Sonia, my first reader and other half.

Chapter 1

S imon Radcliffe-Gould didn't even know why he kept coming back to this gaming hell.

He hadn't the stomach for gambling, not really, and in consequence was very bad at it. He always gave up when he shouldn't and then, inexplicably, dug in his heels when he ought to give up. So he didn't know why, at least once a week, he found himself in this dingy, loud, overdecorated flat in the very northwest corner of London, nearly to Lord's Cricket Ground, losing at cards to men he hadn't even liked much at school.

Well, he did know, actually. It was because of Magdalena da Silva. Definitely the most beautiful woman in London. Probably the most beautiful woman in England. He wouldn't be much surprised if she turned out to be the most beautiful woman in the world. There she was now, laughing at some jest of Meyer Henney's, her obnoxious lover and host of the establishment.

Her laughter lit up the dim room like sunlight, purifying the London soot and dust into country air. Her skin was golden in the candlelight, her brown hair piled on her head, mostly dark and plain but gleaming here and there like honey. Delight suffused her face so utterly that Simon's chest hurt, a sharp pain like envy or grief or a knife in his heart. She whispered in Henney's ear, and Simon would have sworn that for just a moment her eyes rested on him. A fever of hot and cold pinpricks swept over him.

She and Henney both affected the showy fashions of twenty and thirty years ago, the deep-gaming powder-and-patch days of the *ancien régime*. In Miss da Silva's case, this meant sometimes a great bell of petticoats and sometimes—like tonight—none at all. Even in the candlelight Simon could see the faint outline of her legs.

"My trick." Fletcher swept Simon's five guineas into his pocket. Simon sighed. He should be at home working, not nursing an infatuation with a gambling-den hostess like a student.

If it were his student days and he were here with Clement, Clement would know what to say to her. He would have already made her laugh, bribed her, and dropped her in Simon's lap like a gift. Maybe he would have leaned in and whispered in Simon's ear, *We'll share her.*

Simon burned at the thought, and it was only about a third lust and a third resentment and inadequacy. The last third was a longing still violent enough to feel like homesickness, even now after three years apart. He felt in his pocket for Clement's letter.

I want you to design a folly for Throckmorton, to celebrate my accession. Something cheerful to mark a sad occasion. Can you come next week? I'm having a small house party, but I promise we won't bother you.

Unfortunately, Simon knew what that promise was worth.

Absolutely nothing.

"Well?" Bishop asked impatiently. Simon realized the other players thought he was reaching in his pocket for his next stake, not dithering over an invitation for next week.

He withdrew his hand, pushing himself up from his chair. "I'll watch the play this round, I think."

"I've no more ready money." Henney's Dutch-accented voice rang out from across the room. "Let's make it interesting."

Simon's stomach flipped. Everyone in the room knew what Henney meant by *Let's make it interesting*. It meant, *I'm going to stake my mistress, because I'm a base, caddish, hateful muckworm with no respect for a woman.* And somehow, when Henney staked Miss da Silva, he always lost. Probably didn't bother to exert himself, when he stood to lose no money.

Miss da Silva moved obediently to stand behind Henney's chair, but as she did, Simon swore her eyes met his again. The message in them was clear: *Save me from this brute.* He started forward, determined to put a stop to this, and her face lit up hopefully.

But then she turned away, leaning upon the back of Henney's chair and smiling at his opponent, Lord Sinclair. Giving in.

The club's furniture had been rescued from the dust heaps of the last century, and somewhere Henney had dug up a dozen mismatched voyeuse chairs, built with a third armrest topping the back so a friend could watch one's play over one's shoulder. The host liked to sit in the softest, largest, most throne-like of them, a great Louis XV wing chair of worn turquoise velvet. Miss da Silva laid one gloved arm on the cushion, deliberately pillowing her breasts on it.

You don't have to play his games, Simon thought at her. *You don't have to offer yourself up at the snap of his fingers.*

She cut her eyes at Simon again, and this time it was pure flirtation. His stomach flipped again, that she'd surrendered so completely. "I've just remembered an urgent appointment," he said, though it was nearly two in the morning, and fled.

Not long after, Simon crawled into bed alone. It was the warmest summer in years, but the sheets were still chilly everywhere the warming-pan hadn't touched. He tried to remember the last time he'd shared a bed with someone. If Magdalena da Silva were here, he wouldn't be so damned lonely.

Simon was so lonely he felt like a blown-out eggshell.

He had to stop thinking about her. He had to stop going to her boring club. She lived with Henney, and unless—*unless you win her at piquet,* he thought, and hated himself for it.

He had to get out of town. He needed work, and Clement was offering him a commission. He could think of ten different wonderful places to put a folly on the Throckmorton grounds, and he hadn't seen Clement since Lord Throckmorton's funeral three months ago. He'd even avoided answering most of his letters, because he was a terrible, ungenerous friend. He should go. Clement would be occupied with his guests anyway, and Simon could spend most of his time working.

He shouldn't go. Clement had tried to kiss him after the funeral. He'd begged Simon to stay the night. *It doesn't have to mean anything.*

He'd just been upset. It was his father's funeral, after all.

Simon had been very firm, *again*, that all that was over for good. Surely Clement would behave himself this time. He had a new lover, he'd mentioned in one of his letters. Hopefully that would distract him.

It wasn't as if Simon could just never visit him again. Clement was his best friend.

He wanted to get out of bed right then and write his acceptance letter, before he could dither over it any more. But it was chilly, and he'd have to light the candle with his tinder-box, and his valet would see him, and he couldn't post it until the morning anyway.

So instead, he lay there and dithered.

"So how was Sinclair?" Meyer asked over breakfast in their little room behind the club.

"Mmm." Maggie stretched, sore in all the right places. "Very masterful."

Meyer smiled lazily. "Just how you like them."

Maggie stirred marmalade into her tea. "Mm-hmm." Meyer himself was one of the most masterful men she knew, though she didn't know how many people would recognize it, looking at him with his shaggy hair uncombed and his ancient brocade dressing gown trailing in the butter. Most people would discount him only for his height; he topped Maggie by no more than an inch or two.

But most people didn't understand that size and strength didn't make a man masterful. In bed, Meyer's quiet confidence—sometimes nearing implacable indifference to others' opinions—manifested itself as a careless ruthlessness that enchanted her.

Still, variety was the spice of life, and Meyer never begrudged her a night with one of Number Eighteen's patrons. They made a game of it, him contriving to lose her at piquet to a man of her choosing. Maggie loved feeling like an object to be bartered, loved the casual exercise of power, loved playing at obedient surrender while carnal possibility built in the air, the cards sliding against each other with soft caressing sounds. And it got the man in the right frame of mind to swagger and bully her a little.

"I told you I wanted Simon Radcliffe-Gould, though."

Meyer paused in spreading poppyseed preserves on his toast to roll his eyes. "Why?"

Maggie frowned at him. "What do you mean? Because he's beautiful."

If his eyes could have actually left his head and wandered up to the ceiling, they would have. "In a chinless *goyishe* sort of way."

"I like his chin!"

"You would."

Despite Meyer's teasing, Mr. Radcliffe-Gould's jaw was definitely there, in a sharp delicate way Maggie felt in her bones. His pallor didn't seem to her to belong to his black hair and dark blue eyes. *Goyishe* she would grant. His mild-featured face was so aristocratically English as to be almost otherworldly. Maybe that was what intrigued her, and gave his beauty its cruel edge—how entirely it shut out little Portuguese Maggie. He would never want her for more than one night, so she wanted that one night, the craving fluttering frantically in her chest like a bat trapped in a chimney.

"He doesn't come in that often," she persisted. "I'm going to miss my chance. *You're* going to miss my chance."

"He's the worst card player in the world. I won't even *pretend* to lose to him at piquet. A man has his pride."

"I can't argue with that," she said, more sharply than she meant to. Meyer's stubbornness might suit her perfectly in bed, but elsewhere, she was a little sick of it.

He relented. "Maybe faro. There's no shame in losing that. A game of pure chance."

"Not the way *you* play it, it isn't."

He grinned wolfishly. "I can't argue with that. You win, Maggie. Next time he comes in, I'll make sure you go home with him."

But he didn't come all the rest of that week. Maggie couldn't help watching for him, her head turning toward the door every time it opened. She suspected her face fell in a pretty impolite manner each time the newcomer wasn't Mr. Radcliffe-Gould.

"Once, you were happy to see me," Meyer mourned, returning from the back room, where he'd gone to change his breeches after a guest overturned a glass of wine. "Ah, love's young dream, so fleeting!" He put his arm around her, smirking. He knew quite well who she was looking for.

Maggie's eyes flew to another new arrival. This time it was only a kid with curly blond hair poking out from under his cap. Yossi, the messenger-boy from Meyer's uncle's counting house. He pushed his way heedlessly through the crowded room, jostling elbows and banging into chairs. Meyer swore and strode forward, expostulating loudly in Yiddish.

Yossi's answer was high-pitched with agitation. He pushed a letter at Meyer, who broke the seal, still scolding—and turned to stone mid-sentence, mouth frozen open.

He shook himself, and more Yiddish followed. Maggie made her way to his elbow. "What is it?" she asked. "What's happened?"

Meyer ignored her. But when she took his arm, he squeezed her hand in a death grip.

At last Yossi nodded and ran out. A card player leaned toward them. "Everything all right, Henney?"

Meyer nodded and clapped him on the back. "Carry on." Not meeting Maggie's eyes, he dragged her into the back room. "My father's dead. I have to go to Rotterdam tomorrow and sit shiva."

Fear speared through her. *For how long? Are you coming back?* She wasn't a good friend.

At least she didn't say it out loud. "I'm so sorry, Meyer. I'll go with you, keep you company."

His mouth tightened. "We can't afford two tickets."

"We'll borrow the money."

He sighed, finally meeting her eyes. You didn't always remember how fine his eyes were; it struck her now. They were large and gray and long-lashed and apologetic. "I can't take you home. You know that. My mother thinks I live alone."

Her heart sank like a stone. The money was an excuse. He didn't want her. She'd only be an encumbrance anyway, someone he had to look after, not speaking the language, not knowing the prayers. Would his mother even accept her as a real Jew?

"I wish I could take you, Maggie. It's going to be a nightmare." He rubbed a hand over his chin. "At least the mirrors will be covered so I won't have to see what I look like after a week without a shave. Ugh, and I'll have to tear one of my coats. Maybe the red one, it's wearing out anyway."

When Meyer was unhappy, he'd ramble restlessly on until someone stopped him. Maggie pushed her hurt feelings aside and wrapped her arms around his waist, resting her chin on his shoulder. He subsided and hugged her back. "It'll only be for a couple of weeks," he mumbled into her neck. "I'll be back before you know it."

I hope so. It was pitiful, to be this afraid to spend a few weeks alone. "I'm so sorry about your father."

He turned his face away. "I haven't seen him in ten years."

She spat his hair out of her mouth. "That doesn't make it easier. You can start packing your trunk, I'll go and send them all away."

Just then, someone from the other room said clearly, "Radcliffe-Gould! Good evening."

Meyer straightened. "I haven't seen my father in ten years. We'll be losing enough profits when I'm gone, no need to start now."

Miss da Silva wasn't here. Why not? She was always here.

How long did Simon have to stay before leaving would seem odd? Half an hour? Or could he get away with twenty minutes?

Then she appeared in the doorway. Henney had her wrist in an iron grip, from which she attempted vainly to free herself. Simon started toward them. To his surprise, Henney dragged her forward and met him halfway, smirking. "Radcliffe-Gould. Care to make things interesting? You can't play piquet to save your life, though. Try faro, you'd have half a chance at winning."

Magdalena's eyes flashed. She leaned in to whisper something in Henney's ear. Simon heard clearly, *Not tonight* and *you lout* and *stay with you*. Simon burned with indignation—and, to his shame, with lust. He had never yet had *Let's make it interesting* directed at him. He had never wanted to.

Not...with his mind, anyway. He'd hated that the thought crept in, sometimes. *She'd have to do whatever I wanted.* Which was filthy, disgusting nonsense.

Up close, her beauty was overwhelming: wide mouth, long lashes, and large eyes penciled larger. Dimpled elbows showed between her gloves and fanciful overdress, which looked to have been sewn from a Paisley shawl. Did that faint odor of violets and orange-flower water come from her?

Henney ignored her protests. "I'm called away to Rotterdam for a couple of weeks, with nothing in my pocket for expenses. I'll make you a wager. If I win, you pay my way. Say, twenty guineas. If you win, you can borrow Maggie while I'm gone."

She froze—then sighed and gave in. "That means starting tomorrow," she told Simon firmly.

For a moment he was dazzled—a couple of *weeks!*—before common sense asserted itself. "I won't wager for a woman's favors," he said sharply. Let her see that not all men were brutes.

Henney looked him up and down. "Make an exception?"

Miss da Silva put her slender hand on Simon's arm and nodded, very shyly. *Coyly,* he thought, and then scolded himself for self-serving imaginings. "I don't mind," she said. "Honestly."

He allowed himself to put his hand over hers, just for a moment. He would not wager. But perhaps, in the few days between Henney's departure and his own visit to Clement, he might offer to buy her an ice at Gunter's.

The thought of her in sunlight, laughing over a lemon ice with an ancient parasol shading her face and muslin skirts trailing, was almost too much.

"I mind," he said quietly. "I think you do, too."

Henney snorted. "Well, if you're sure you're not interested. Burgoyne!"

Miss da Silva stiffened. "*Meyer.*"

Across the room, Lord Burgoyne stood, eyes on Miss da Silva. Simon, though not well acquainted with the earl, had always liked him, but Magdalena shrank back. "You know I didn't like him," she said in an undertone. "Stop it."

"If Radcliffe-Gould won't wager..." Henney grinned at Simon. "I need to pay my passage somehow."

Miss da Silva wrenched her arm out of Henney's. "This isn't funny."

"Fine," Simon snapped. "I'll wager." It wasn't really a risk he could afford. Twenty guineas was most of what he had in the bank, and the money had to last him until Clement paid for his folly. But he wasn't about to let Miss da Silva go to Burgoyne if she didn't want to. Tomorrow, Henney would be gone. He'd never know if Simon didn't collect on the wager. Miss da Silva might be glad of a fortnight with nobody to please but herself.

Henney kissed Magdalena's cheek. "Don't be angry."

"I'm angry." But after a moment's reluctance, she nestled into him again in a way that made Simon's hand clench into a fist.

Henney led them to a small, unoccupied faro table in the corner. "Count the deck?"

It was impolite to say yes, implying he thought Henney might cheat. But the man was a professional dealer and a cur. Simon held out his hand, and counted. Next Henney shuffled, showily, the cards leaping between his fingers. They were gaining a small audience, two or three peeping Toms who watched Miss da Silva with gleaming eyes. She flushed with embarrassment as she took up the little rake and moved to the croupier's position. Simon wanted to object to their presence, but Henney would only laugh, and anyway there was no practical way to bar onlookers.

"Give him his fish," Henney told Miss da Silva. "Twenty should do."

Taking a box from the locked cupboard in the corner, she counted out twenty ivory fish onto the table before Simon, spilling the rest into the recess in the table provided for the purpose. The fishes' round blank eyes stared hopelessly at him. Simon swallowed hard. He was not very good at faro.

There's nothing to be good at, he scolded himself. *It's a game of pure chance.*

"Mr. Radcliffe-Gould?" Miss da Silva touched his shoulder to get his attention, her fingertips sending sparks up and down his arm. He took the livret of cards she offered, turning them over in his hands. They were a full set of spades from a French deck printed under the Revolution, the court cards showing personifications of Republican virtues. The queen was labeled *Freedom of Marriage*, and in her hand she bore a staff labeled *Divorce*.

Simon stifled a nervous giggle. Where did they *find* these things?

Magdalena's eyes shone proudly. "Aren't they marvelous?"

"They are, rather. Not terribly English, though."

She sighed. "Yes, they're impossible to find here. We scour the secondhand markets. I've heard in Paris you can buy them in every pawnshop."

"Let's make this simple," Henney said. "You double your stake, you win. You lose your stake, you owe me twenty guineas. Seem fair?"

Simon nodded, fighting the impulse to stake all his fish on one card and have it over with. But he was as likely to lose that way as win, and he couldn't give up twenty pounds so quickly.

Of course, in faro you generally *were* as likely to lose as to win. That was why it was so damn popular—better odds than most games of chance. He'd watched Clement play for countless hours, when they were in school. It had felt peaceful when it wasn't his money at stake, cards and coins moving and changing hands, talk washing over him.

Now the cards were in his hands, and it was his money, and it didn't feel peaceful at all. He steeled himself and put six sad, gasping little fish on the figure card with a blue cross, which he remembered dimly indicated a bet on the ace, deuce, and three. One of Miss da Silva's trailing ringlets brushed his arm as she leaned over to inspect his bet.

She did not, it turned out, smell either like orange-flower water *or* violets. Tuberoses burst in his nostrils—heady, carnal, and narcotic. Cloying, even, in the way smells were in bed, arousing *because* they were too strong. He remembered, with great force, that the delicate white blossoms' scent was said to be most powerful at night. He shut his eyes and breathed in.

"I'll lay you a guinea Radcliffe-Gould's cock stands within five pulls," someone said quite audibly.

Pull meant a draw of two cards, one laid to Henney's right and the other to his left. If Simon's bet matched the first card, he lost his stake, and if it matched the second, he won.

But Simon immediately imagined Miss da Silva's hand round his cock.

A laugh. "I'm not taking that bet."

Somehow Simon's humiliation did nothing to lessen his arousal. In some crawling, unwished-for way, it heightened it. Unpleasantly, he remembered lusting after the broad-shouldered senior boy he'd fagged for at Eton, and how every blow and insult had become something resented and relished in equal measure.

Over a decade later, and he was no less easy to bully. He hadn't wanted to take this wager, and Henney had pushed him into it.

The deck slid toward him. "Cut."

He cut, resisting the urge to glance behind him. He could feel watching eyes on the back of his neck. Miss da Silva leaned toward him, murmuring, "Shall I make them go away?"

Simon looked up in surprise. She felt for *his* embarrassment? Yet she did seem less embarrassed than he felt. It pained him, that she valued herself so little. "You don't belong to him, you know," he whispered. "You don't have to go with either me or Burgoyne. You could simply *go*."

She blinked and pulled back. "So could you. I'm fine where I am."

"Play," Henney said loudly. The soda card—the first draw, that counted for naught—was an ace. None of Simon's cards came up in the first pull. Next a pair of deuces were turned over, meaning he lost half his stake. Miss da Silva slid three of his fish into Henney's bank with a rattle.

The odds of low cards turning up was lower now that three had gone by, so Simon switched his bet to court cards. When a queen flashed in Henney's hand, his heart pounded triumphantly—but it was the losing card.

He was down to twelve fish now. How could a game where you had more or less a straight fifty percent chance of losing your money be considered good odds? Why was gambling considered good fun at all?

He put another two fish on the court cards. They went too, Henney's voice smug as he called the pulls in a loud, clear voice. Ten fish left.

Miss da Silva plucked one of his fish from the table and kissed it. "For luck."

A small smear of crimson lip salve clung to the fish when she set it down. Simon could not take his eyes off it. *For luck.* Did she want him to win? Surely she'd rather have his twenty guineas for her household than spend a fortnight earning her keep in his bed.

He passed quickly over that image, beginning his thought again: she must want the money…unless it went into Henney's pocket and never came back out. Did she *need* another keeper in his absence?

His stake was split with Henney again for a pair, the fish with her lip salve on it clinking into the bank. He should have kept that one for last.

"Good thing I didn't take that bet," an onlooker said behind him. Simon burned with humiliation, but his cock only grew harder.

Good God, this was ridiculous. Twenty guineas would be a small price to pay to put this madness behind him. He clenched his jaw and pushed all his remaining fish, nine of them, onto Freedom of Marriage.

Henney smiled. "Ready to lose?"

Miss da Silva reached out to brush some lint from the baize table. Her paste ring caught the light in a blaze, and Simon blinked and looked away, missing the draw.

"Three—well, damn," Henney said, startled. "Queen." Simon looked, and there was the queen of hearts smiling at him from the stack of cards to Henney's left.

Miss da Silva smiled, counting out nine tokens. Simon was...almost back to where he'd started. Wonderful.

"Do you want to cock it?" In polite society, one called doubling one's bet at faro *paroli*, not *cocking*. But Miss da Silva used the vulgar term without hesitation. Suggestively, even. Behind him, the watchers sniggered. For a moment, he couldn't help lumping her in with them. Mocking him, trying to make him uncomfortable for the sake of it.

He wasn't a shy adolescent any more. What did he care what any of them thought? And what was he ashamed of, exactly? He'd done nothing wrong. He wasn't going to do anything wrong. Even if they told his mother—

He smothered a laugh at that. He definitely did not want them to tell his mother. The laughter calmed him enough that he could smile up at Miss da Silva. "You have no idea how much."

Her breath caught. Her breath actually caught, the old-fashioned ruffle at her low neckline fluttering. Tuberose wafted toward him.

"Give him a taste of what he'll be getting," Henney suggested.

Simon's first thought was, *It's a little enough thing to take, when I don't mean to take anything else.* But one did not expect a return for a good deed, and one certainly did not demand one. He refused to be in league with Henney, over anything. Even if he wanted to go home with a smear of her lip salve on his mouth.

She leaned toward him.

"That won't be necessary." His voice came out a little rough. "I have a good imagination." For a moment, self-indulgently, he let himself believe she looked disappointed.

Turning her face away, she cocked up the corner of his card to show that he doubled his bet.

"Five, queen," Henney called. "It's your lucky night, Radcliffe-Gould."

Thirty-six fish now sat in a yellowish pile before Simon. Almost enough to win.

"*Sept et le va?*" Miss da Silva asked.

Simon couldn't remember what that was. *Sept* was seven. He'd have eight times his original stake if he left his money on the queen and won again, wouldn't he? But his winnings minus his stake...*that* would be seven times...? "Why not?" he said recklessly.

She leaned forward and cocked up another corner of the card, so it did mean venturing all again. He shouldn't. The odds were against another queen so soon. Weren't they? There was only one queen left in the deck.

"Five guineas says he loses it all," someone said.

"Another five says if he does, he goes straight out and finds a whore."

"Ten," Henney called, turning the card over.

"How would we know if he did or not?"

"And...queen." Henney laughed disbelievingly. "Well, never let it be said I was ungracious in defeat."

And that was it. Simon had won.

Miss da Silva bent down and brushed her lips to his. Tuberoses filled his nostrils, ringlets tickled his neck, and her lips...well, he supposed all he could say about them at this juncture was *soft* and *warm*. But they were very soft and very warm, and—

He imagined her lips around his cock. Oh God. At this rate how would he walk home? He certainly had no intention of finding a whore. The awkwardness of that usually outweighed the pleasure. He glanced around the room to see if there was anyone he knew from school who might oblige him. No such luck.

"I'll see you tomorrow," she said.

"What time shall I call for you? I..." He glanced coldly at Henney. "I should prefer to find you alone."

Miss da Silva stepped back.

"I shall take the mail, to be sure of not missing my boat,"

Henney said. The mail coaches left Piccadilly late in the evening. "But I'll be out on errands most of the day. If you come and fetch her between noon and two, I'll engage to be out of the way."

Simon stood, silently cursing the fashion for cutaway coats. There was nothing to hide the erection poking at his breeches. Certainly Miss da Silva's eyes went there straight-away. She gulped and flushed with—well, it might have been apprehension. It might have been shared mortification.

Eagerness, he thought, but it was a self-serving notion.

He bowed over her hand with as much aplomb as he could manage. "Until tomorrow, Miss da Silva."

Chapter 2

At half past eleven, Maggie kissed Meyer and saw him out the door. Then the waiting began. She could not stop thinking of Mr. Radcliffe-Gould's cock tenting his breeches, and the husky note in his voice as he wished her goodnight. For all his good manners and better morals, he wanted her. He wanted this.

Had he been thinking of her all night, too? Perhaps he would take her right here in the parlor. It would have to be against the wall, for she and Meyer had discovered already to their sorrow that the card tables could not be relied on to take the weight. She shut her eyes, enjoying the delicious ache between her legs.

A knock came at the door. She flew to let him in.

She had never seen Mr. Radcliffe-Gould in morning dress before. In the sunlight blazing through the open windows, his blue coat turned his eyes the color of lapis. Her mouth went dry at the way the buttons on his pantaloon legs pulled the buff fabric tight around his calves. His plain white waistcoat was spotless and his top-boots shone.

She knew a moment of embarrassment at how dingy the card-room looked in daylight: scratched tables, stained carpet, and pale, streaky wallpaper. Mr. Radcliffe-Gould must be used to places that gleamed twenty-four hours a day. Even her favorite striped jacket felt faded and foolish, its wide lapels and enormous buttons antiquated and every snagged thread painfully visible.

"Good afternoon," he said. "May I come in?"

She nodded hastily and stepped back. "Please, sit. Would you like some tea?" Oh, why had she said that? It would hardly hasten amorous advances.

"I would love some, thank you."

She hurried to fetch out the tea-tray. She might have simply invited him into the back room, but—that was private. "I'm afraid the tea isn't very hot anymore," she said defeatedly. "But the biscuits are very good. They're from the Portuguese bakery." She nibbled at one herself. This was definitely not what she'd imagined.

"Please don't be nervous," he said gently. "I assure you, I don't mean to hold you to anything. A promise made under duress cannot be considered binding."

"What?" She sprayed biscuit crumbs everywhere.

"I'm going out of town in a few days myself. To a friend's house in the country. Perhaps you'll enjoy a week or two of freedom from the demands of men."

"I can't stay here by myself!"

His narrow lips curved into a half-smile. "Why not?"

She wanted to put her hands right on his gold-buttoned chest and give him a good shove. "I've never lived alone. I can't sleep for listening to noises." Besides, Meyer had befriended a dozen old-clothes men in his quest to own every embroidered waistcoat in London. Maggie didn't mind them coming by now and then for a cup of tea or a piece of toast—except for old Mr. Jacobs, who wasn't very nice—but with Meyer out of the country every knock at the door would frighten her. She took a deep breath. "Is that really what you want? I know Meyer bullied you into the wager, but I thought... Well, it seemed plain enough you wanted me." Why couldn't she say *cock* to him, suddenly?

He flushed a delicate pink. He was ashamed to want her. She was too low for him. Her breasts ached with unhappy arousal. *Take me just once, and be bitterly ashamed of it.*

"A gentleman may want something, and not take it. Not every man is like Henney."

She was on her feet, shaking. "What is that supposed to mean?"

He stood too, obviously startled. "Anyone can see how he treats you. Bartering you whenever he runs out of cash—"

"*Anyone* could see that was a game, if they paid attention!" She brushed crumbs angrily from her skirts. "Meyer has never taken a thing from me I wasn't panting for him to take, so wipe that sneer off your face. He learned his *father* died last night and he still looked out for me before anything. If you only came here to carp at my dearest friend in the world, I can—" She stopped short. What *was* she to do? No one she knew had space for a house guest. She'd been so relieved last night not to have to worry about it. She glared at him resentfully. "I suppose you'll be spending a fortnight in a house with a hundred empty feather beds while I'm sleeping on my mother's floor. What a gentleman you are, to be sure!"

Simon tried to remember the last time he'd felt this morti-
fied. He was nauseous with it. Even last night did not come
close. "A game," he repeated. Of *course* it was a game. She *had*
been coy, and eager, and all the things he'd told himself he
was uncharitably imagining. He'd been fancying her a poor
wronged woman, and instead she was only another free-
spirited sophisticate. "What a fool you must have thought me."

"I thought you were sweet," she snapped. "Which makes
me the fool, I believe."

He pressed his lips tightly together. "Why me?"

She crossed her arms over her chest. "Because Meyer knew
I liked you." Her scowl softened suddenly. "Oh, and maybe he
remembered I don't like staying alone!" For a moment she
seemed buoyed up by Henney's kindness, but she deflated
quickly, flapping a hand at him. "I'm sorry we embarrassed
you. Why don't you just go?"

Meyer knew I liked you. She was so beautiful, and charming, and she'd picked him out of everybody in that room?

Don't be flattered, he told himself sternly. *Remember how
flattered you always were that Clement liked you.*

The worst of it was, this was the merest taste of what he'd
be in for at Clement's little house party. People trying to draw
him into their smug little games, happy and jolly and completely oblivious that other people would prefer to keep to
themselves. People urging him to waste his money and telling
him in a superior tone how much he *wanted* things he'd only
done because it would have been more trouble to say no.

Would he say no, if Clement kissed him again? He *did*
want Clement, after all. Or his heart did, stupidly, and his
body, when his brain had long since stopped.

The truth was, he knew he wouldn't let Clement kiss him. But the odds were probably about even as to whether Simon would actually turn him out of the room—which Clement would have a key to, since it was his house—or let him stay until the early morning explaining how unhappy Simon was making him. The odds were even that Clement would end up in tears, too. As bad a bet as faro.

Miss da Silva made another restless gesture with one beautiful hand, her ring catching the light. Suddenly he remembered how that flash had made him look away from the deal last night. She and Henney between them had card-sharped him!

It was a crime and he should be appalled, but he wasn't particularly. Instead he thought, *If only I could somehow do the same to Clement...*

Maybe he could.

"Let's make a new deal," he suggested. *Clement won't be happy.* His stomach churned a little, but he ignored it. "You come with me to my house party and pretend to be my mistress."

She blinked. "You can bring a mistress with you to a house party?"

"It's..." He sighed. "It's not a respectable house party. I imagine there'll be a lot of...goings-on. I'm there to work, but I know they'll try to drag me into things. And I really just want to get my job done. So you pretend to be my mistress and give me an excuse to leave a room whenever I like, and you can be assured of good food, excellent wine, and a feather bed for two weeks." He started to smile. This would work brilliantly.

Her mouth twisted, considering. "Are you sure you only

want me to *pretend*?" she said rather plaintively.

No. "Yes," he said firmly.

She sighed. "Are your friends amusing?"

No, he almost said, but Clement was very amusing, and while Simon usually disliked his other friends, they were probably her kind of people. "Yes."

"It's a bargain, then." She held out her bare hand. Simon shook it, wishing passionately that he wasn't wearing gloves. Maybe this wasn't as good an idea as it had seemed half a minute ago.

Too late now.

"So what are the rules?" Miss da Silva asked. "When we're in company, can I kiss you or hang on you to shore up our pretense? Or should I keep my distance?"

"Let me think about it a moment." Simon's voice emerged about an octave higher than usual.

She sat beside him in a rented post chaise, wearing a sea of white muslin dotted with tiny whorls of spangles and hemmed with more glittering greenery. She *had* also been sporting a striped redingote and an enormous straw hat in a style Simon's mother had dismissed at the time as "Puritans at the seaside," but despite the open windows it was so hot in the chaise that she'd given up and exposed her muslin and her carefully curled hair to the dust. She looked playful and seductive, and she spoke so matter-of-factly. Simon wanted her to kiss and hang on him. In company and out. She could start by sitting in his lap right now.

He was conscious that he himself had spent rather a long time in front of the mirror this morning. He'd tied his cravat in one of the fancy knots he hadn't bothered with in ages. He and Clement used to practice them for hours, to the despair of their laundress.

Hopefully Clement wouldn't think Simon had chosen the cravat for *him*. The knot had an unfortunately sensual name, he remembered suddenly.

But he was crawlingly conscious that he *had* partly dressed for Clement. Oh, he wanted nothing more than for Clement not to desire him anymore. It would make everything so much easier, not least for Clement himself, and yet...the idea of Clement thinking him unattractive made him a little queasy. As if he would *be* unattractive, if Clement thought so.

And Clement would know. He would look at Simon and he would know.

Shoring up their pretense was an excellent idea. "One or two kisses in the first few days should suffice," he said. "You may hang on me as much as you like."

Miss da Silva's smiling face caught the sun from the carriage window. "And what name shall I call you?"

He had somehow, even in his darkest imaginings, failed to comprehend how dangerously tempting this charade would be. "Simon."

"And you must call me Maggie."

He couldn't help smiling back. "I'd like that."

"And..." She traced one of the spangled curlicues on her gown with her finger. "When we're alone. Shall I keep my distance then?"

He looked away, out the front window, but as that placed

the well-developed arse of the postilion squarely in his view, it did less to calm him than he'd hoped. "I'd appreciate it if you would."

"Why? I'm not trying to talk you into changing your mind, I promise. But I don't understand. I like you, and I think—I think you like me, and it isn't as if I'm asking you to marry me. Only for us to enjoy each other's company for a couple of weeks." There was a slight nervous vibrato in her voice. He was so flattered that she cared enough to be nervous, and he wanted to make her happy, and God knew he wanted to enjoy her company. He almost gave in.

"I'm five-and-twenty," he said slowly. "I'm not seeking to enjoy myself. I'm trying to be sensible and earn a living. I'm making a go of things as an architect."

"Don't you design follies?"

Why couldn't anyone believe he was really working? *Maybe because your last commission was four months ago, and after renting this carriage you have less than twenty pounds to your name,* a voice suggested. "I didn't say I was a Quaker!" he snapped. "And there's nothing really foolish about follies. They're ornamental buildings, that's all. Times are difficult, and they provide work for idle men. I always encourage my clients to use local stone, so there's quarrying, hauling, and building all to enrich the district."

Her smile was skeptical.

"Beauty has its place too, and joy. What's the purpose of that dress, when a sack would do as well?"

The contrary woman looked pleased. "You like my dress."

"Of course I like your dress. And I like you, too," he admitted. "But I do, actually, want to find someone who'll ask me to

marry them." That wasn't entirely true, since he was as likely
to find himself wishing to spend his life with a man as with
a woman. "Settle down with, anyway. Not someone to drink
and play cards with and dress outrageously and shock people
for the sake of it and come into my room in the middle of the
night because you ate too much opium, sobbing and demanding I tell you I love you over and over again for five hours when
we have exams the next day!"

Maggie's eyes were lovely green saucers.

Simon could not quite manage to regret his reckless honesty. One didn't reveal such a thing by accident, not when one
had always had to be careful. He did want to be honest with
her. Maybe not even with *her*. Maybe this carriage, hurtling
across England, was a small square of liberty between two
places where he had to be careful, and he wanted to enjoy it to
the fullest. "I've done that," he said, feeling tired and strangely
peaceful. "You seem to think I'm the height of respectability,
but my name was linked with a wild crowd at school. Some of
the people we're going to see, in fact. And I'm through with it."

He just wished he'd managed to find a new crowd to
replace them.

She leaned thoughtfully against the squabs. "I'm seven-
and-twenty, you know. Older than you. I've been done with
that kind of Cheltenham tragedy for a long time now. I only
mention it because I resent your implication that that's how I
live. Of course I'll keep my distance, since you wish it."

"Thank you." He hesitated. "Please be discreet. I suppose
it's obvious I wasn't talking about a woman, just now." He was
trying to earn his living now, and one never knew whom it
would matter to.

"My lips are sealed," she said at once. "Don't all English gentlemen do that at school, though? There aren't any women, after all."

Simon's nerves jangled. "I suppose." He hadn't ruled out continuing to do it after school. He liked it just as well as the other. That was the difference.

She nodded. "Thank you for trusting me."

I don't, he thought, but he didn't say it.

"I'm sorry you and he couldn't sort things out. Love should be easier than it is."

"We could never have sorted things out. We were too different." Unexpectedly, his eyes stung. He hadn't felt different from Clement at the time. They'd met mounting a production of *Antony and Cleopatra* at Eton. Simon had managed the scenery, and Clement, of course, had been Cleopatra. Simon had been moved to tears at every rehearsal of the death scene, and Clement had admired his scenery, and that had been that. *Like two peas in a pod,* his mother had said when he brought Clement home.

If he saw that scenery now, he'd cringe at its lack of historical authenticity. But he couldn't shake the belief that thirteen-year-old Clement would make him cry all over again with *As sweet as balm, as soft as air, as gentle—O Antony!*

"Do you want children?" she asked, tracing spangles again, and then gave a frustrated jerk of her head. "I'm sorry, that was awfully rude. I didn't ask because of—I meant because of what you said about settling down. I wasn't thinking."

"Yes. I think it would be nice." He'd daydreamed about it more than he'd care to admit, actually. One could always foster someone else's child, if one's own was not available. "Do you?"

he asked, since he thought when she said, *I wasn't thinking,* she had meant, *I was thinking of myself.*

"Yes," she said quietly.

"Does Henney know that?"

She shook her head. "I don't...can *you* be discreet?"

He leaned forward, thrilled to know something about her that Henney didn't, despite his resolve to keep his distance. "I'm a closet lock and key of villainous secrets."

"I don't want... No, I'm sorry, I can't tell you."

"That's unsportsmanlike of you."

"You'll think it's a criticism of Meyer. And you already don't like him, and it *isn't* one."

"You don't want to have children with him," he guessed.

"He doesn't want to have children with me either," she insisted. "It isn't anything wrong with him! We're only... I don't know. We aren't right for each other that way. We couldn't raise a child together. We'd quarrel over everything."

Simon sympathized. He himself had always suspected that Clement would be a fair-weather kind of guardian. Simon would have always had to deal with tears and mete out punishment.

She sighed. "It's my mother's fondest dream that I marry him, and he'll go back to clerking for his uncle, and we'll have nice lodgings in the City and eight children."

"Does she have any reason to think this might come to pass?"

"He offered once." She gave a rueful half-smile. "I thought I might be increasing. And he was very kind about it! But he was also very relieved when my courses came. My mother, on the other hand, was very disappointed."

That was one terror Simon had been spared by confining his youthful adventures mostly to boys. "How did *you* feel?"

"I was relieved *and* disappointed." She looked determinedly out the window, seeming to regret having let the conversation become so personal. "And do you want to tell them all the truth, about how we met, and why I'm here? Not the whole truth, I mean, but...the faro game?"

"It would be pointless to lie. There were a lot of people at the club that night. No one will think anything of it, I assure you."

She nodded briskly. "One last question. You said it's to be a rather scandalous party. If somebody else invites me to his bed, do you care how I answer him? Will it affect your standing with your friends?"

Was she really asking his permission to bed his friends? Couldn't she go two weeks without fucking somebody? He'd gone most of a year now with no noticeable ill effects. However, it was none of his affair and he certainly had no right to demand fidelity.

"You may do as you please in the daytime. But I'd appreciate it if you would spend the nights with me. And...if anyone troubles you, or importunes you more than you'd like, you must tell me at once, and I'll deal with it."

She didn't laugh, as he'd been half-afraid she would. "Thank you. Can you think of anything else we ought to discuss?"

He couldn't, and she gave her attention to the scenery, evidently setting herself to be cheerful. "I haven't spent much time in the country. Well, I suppose I live in Marylebone now. I grew up in Lisbon and the East End, so that nearly qualifies as rural. Meyer and I have toured the grand houses in Richmond and Hounslow a few times, too. But you can't even *see* a house from here. Living in the middle of nowhere must be terribly dull after a while, but it's so pretty." She knelt on the seat to stick her head out the side window, leaning dangerously farther and farther out. Alarmed, Simon steadied her. Her hips felt more solid than he'd expected inside all those petticoats, wide and curving...

"Thanks," she shouted.

When the postilion turned round to see what the noise was about, she gave him a friendly wave, and he grinned at her. What was it like to be so easy with people?

She popped back inside the carriage. "Just a moment, I want to take my hair down." Honey-and-walnut waves did not precisely tumble over her breasts—they just brushed the upper curve of her bosom and, like all hair just let down, hung in frizzing hanks, rather. Simon was overcome anyway.

She dove back out the window. "Hold me tight, I'm going to let go!"

He seized her round the waist, and she threw her arms wide, shrieking with delight as her hair whipped about her face. "Faster!" she urged the postilion, who bent low over his horse and obliged her.

Which left Simon the only person not having fun. He supposed there was nothing to stop him pulling her back inside and taking a turn himself, except that it was dangerous and stupid and he wouldn't trust her not to drop him.

He was so tired of being sensible and not enjoying himself, and somehow ending up doing stupid things anyway.

Clement bounded down the Throckmorton steps and kissed Simon full on the mouth. Simon tensed at the unexpectedness of it. But of course: Clement had seen Maggie dutifully hanging on Simon's arm and wanted to assert himself.

"Pardon me, I'm terribly old-fashioned," he said with a wave in Simon's direction. "Did you know in our grandfathers' time it was considered positively *French* to kiss on the cheek?" He looked very handsome in his mourning, romantically pale and only a little wilted in the summer heat.

Simon felt a pang of loss, that the scent of Clement's soap and the familiar press of his lips—chapped a little from the sun—could produce such overwhelming annoyance.

Maggie, though, gave every appearance of being charmed. "I didn't know that! I enjoy an antique flourish myself, as you can see." Her curtsey showed off her billowing skirts.

"Miss da Silva, may I present Mr.—I mean, the Viscount Throckmorton."

"A pleasure, Lord Throckmorton."

Clement, obviously noting the dust on her glove, did not take old-fashioned manners farther than a kiss in the air several inches above it. "Good Lord, Simon, I thought you were taking a closed carriage."

"May I speak to you a moment, Throckmorton?"

"Of course, Radcliffe-Gould." Clement drew him happily into a corner of the hall. His eyes ran up and down Simon, lingering on that damn cravat knot. Simon flushed. "I'm so glad you could come down. I had them bring up your favorite wines for dinner, the 1805 Verdelho and—"

Simon almost gave up. Clement was in a good mood, and he took everything so hard that it always felt cruel to confront him. *I'm glad I could come down too,* he could say.

But in the end, he *couldn't* say it. "What if I hadn't told her?"

"Told her what?"

"You know what." For a long, silent moment he thought Clement might really pretend not to know. If he did, the pressure in Simon's head might actually levitate his hat.

"But you did tell her, evidently, so there's no harm done."

He tried to say it gently. "I didn't tell her about you, because I thought you might like some choice in the matter."

The happiness drained out of Clement's face. His mouth shrank in on itself, almost disappearing.

Simon's stomach churned. "Clement, please don't sulk."

"I just got carried away. I was happy to see you."

"No you weren't." *You were jealous.* But he would deny that too, and Simon would feel so angry, and Clement would be hurt, and what was the point? He was stuck here until he could design a folly. He should let it roll off him, like water from a duck's back. Why couldn't he ever do that? Instead, Clement's sadness clung to his skin and dug balefully in.

"Are you even happy to see me anymore?" Clement asked in a small voice, fidgeting with one cuff.

He had been. That was the worst of it. Even now part of Simon wanted to set all this nonsense aside and talk about the book he was reading, and the sheet music he'd bought, and the funny thing the girl at the shop said that morning.

And if he did, Clement would think it meant something it didn't. "Of course I am," he said, feeling as if the words were drawn out with pincers. "I'm always happy to see you. You know that."

The moment hung in the air as Clement decided whether to push it. Then he smiled, relaxing. "I do, I'm sorry, I'm just being silly and thin-skinned. Now tell me all about Miss da Silva. She's too pretty and Continental. How did you meet her?"

"I won her in a game of faro, actually." Simon did his best not to preen hypocritically about it, even when Clement whistled.

Simon had already given a great deal of thought to the fact that he and Maggie would be sharing a room. He had imagined the darkness, and the sound of her breathing, and how he would have to stay turned resolutely on his side to keep from touching her.

He'd imagined the bed so vividly he'd forgotten about dressing and undressing. Now here she was in shift and stays and a clean sprigged petticoat, fussing over her wardrobe like a mother hen with her chicks. She'd brought two enormous trunks of clothes with her, insisting they were necessary both for the charade and to prevent them from being stolen in her absence. "I'm sorry, I know I'm disgustingly particular," she told the maid who'd come up with the trunks. "But all these petticoats have got to be hung up, and not pressed all together either." Maggie darted a ruthless smile at Simon. "If you've got to squash something, squash *his* things."

The maid smiled hesitantly, unwilling to risk annoying Simon.

The threat to his clothes did not annoy him. Nor did it

annoy him that it looked as if a muslin factory had exploded over half the bed. Spangles, embroidery, stripes...all of which Maggie ignored to set out her hairpins on the dressing table, and her hairbrush and jewelry. Unwinding a shawl from around a little painted cut-glass perfume bottle, she set the bottle by the mirror as carefully as if it were a Crown Jewel. Simon felt dizzy, remembering the scent of tuberoses.

Men were *supposed* to be annoyed at being surrounded by a froth of femininity, weren't they? But he wasn't sure why. In this case *froth* was not a strong enough word—the room was rapidly becoming a whipped custard, a meringue, or perhaps a many-layered trifle of femininity—and Simon just wanted to roll her into that cloud of muslin and kiss her.

But he had resolved with himself not to. *That* was what annoyed him.

He stood awkwardly by the right side of the bed—*his* side, he supposed, as she'd left it mostly empty. Even dusty and hot as he was, he hesitated to remove his clothes. Ridiculous, when she stood there in her corset, a ladder of thin drawstrings shaping each breast. Like her hips, her bosom was more generous than it had looked beneath gowns and gauze kerchiefs.

At last Simon took off his coat. His sleeves emerged, wrinkled and sweaty. He dug through his trunk for a fresh shirt. Dinner, damn, they'd have to go to dinner. That meant evening clothes. His evening coat was a mess of wrinkles.

A soupçon of tuberoses told him she was beside him. "Oh, dear. Remind me when we leave, and I'll show you how to fold your coats for traveling. Doesn't your valet know better?" The maid seemed to have departed, probably with a tax-roll's worth of instructions.

Simon had a valet only in the loosest sense of the word. The man's talents extended to grilling a steak, answering the postman's knock, and carrying a basket to the laundress, and there stopped. "Obviously not."

Her little grimace drew attention to her full lips. "I can see why you left him at home."

"I left him at home because I didn't want to make him ride on the outside of the carriage, or waste a fortnight being poked at by the stuck-up menservants of our fellow guests. I can do for myself well enough, and if I can't, Clement will lend me his man."

She giggled.

"What?"

"He'll *lend* you his *man*," she repeated drolly, making a juvenile double entendre of the words. "I thought you didn't approve of that sort of thing."

"I never said I didn't approve," he said evenly. "I just said I wasn't interested. People should do what makes them happy. At least—to be honest, I do think people ought to avoid liaisons with their servants." He felt sad, and annoyed, and tired. "Miss da Silva, I'm going to spend the next two weeks with people telling me I'm a stick-in-the-mud, and imagining I disapprove of them because I don't want to join in whatever little game they happen to be playing. I'd rather not face it in my own room, if you don't mind. Haven't you ever just *not wanted* to do something?"

She took a step back, the odor of tuberoses fading, and he wished he hadn't said anything. "I'm sorry. Of course. I didn't mean...I don't think you're a stick-in-the-mud."

"Oh no?"

When she shook her head, a bit of road dust drifted down to her bare shoulder. Without thinking, he leaned forward and blew it off.

She shivered. Her breast was inches from his eye as he drew back, golden and his for the taking. Why wasn't he taking it, again?

"I think you know what you want, and you hold fast to it," she said. "Some people can't manage to do either. *I* can't, sometimes. I admire it."

That was a joke. This whole damn house party was a joke, in fact. Simon knew what he wanted, all right: the absolute worst thing for himself, as always. First Clement, now her, and in between, a thousand reckless extravagances of the heart and pocketbook. He was five-and-twenty, an adult, a man of business, and paying Henney's passage to Rotterdam would have emptied his bank account.

She was a creature of extravagance from first to last. He couldn't afford her.

Chapter 3

Simon evaluated the crowd at dinner. Three women and seven men, counting himself and Maggie. The other two women were courtesans, brought in both to oblige the guests and to provide them with cover. The men were mostly Clement's usual awkward assortment: Reggie Skeffington, with a knack for always saying the wrong thing and not noticing he'd done so; Danny St. Aubyn, a gangly, brown-skinned young man fond of enthusiastically recounting amusing anecdotes about his own misadventures; Harry Palliser, who got into so many irritating arguments that no one wanted to talk to him; and Geoff Trollope, who mostly stayed quiet and laughed pleasantly at other people's jokes. Simon didn't hate any of them and actually liked St. Aubyn and Sir Geoff, so all in all, it might have been worse. Most of them were in love with Clement, but everybody was at one point or another.

Clement had once confided that when he was a little boy, he'd always befriended the children no one else liked, because he thought they'd never abandon him. Simon hadn't pointed out that Clement still did the same thing.

A few days afterward, it had occurred to him extremely painfully that perhaps Clement had chosen him on the same principle. He tried not to think about that.

Aloysius Darling, Clement's new lover, must have been chosen for his looks, because he didn't fit in with the others at all. He was by far the oldest man in the room, probably over forty, with curly blond hair and a smile so pleased with himself that it bordered on the beatific. Simon hated him already. He was currently arguing a red-faced Palliser into a corner for the fun of it, about something he obviously did not care a jot about himself. St. Aubyn was trying in vain to distract them with a story about setting himself on fire while making toast, which had Geoff in stitches. Clement was not trying to rein his lover in at all; instead, he was trying to attract his attention by talking loudly to Simon, who he'd put on his other side.

Simon sighed and tried to talk mostly to Maggie. Unfortunately, she wasn't saying much.

Maggie never felt shy at Number Eighteen. She was never intimidated there by titles, or Mayfair accents, or ruddy English faces. She even felt sorry for them sometimes, bleeding money in elegantly bland little clusters, eager for scraps of her and Meyer's glamor and daring.

Here, in the lofty-ceilinged dining room of an English country house, not knowing where to put her elbows as footmen leaned past her to remove and place platters for course after course, she felt like a brightly colored bug who'd flown in the window by mistake, at once insignificant and conspicuous.

She wondered if the other women, who'd introduced themselves to her as an Italian opera dancer and an Irish brothel girl, felt self-conscious too. If so, they didn't show it.

Maybe they'd been places like this before.

These houses had seemed like museums when she and Meyer toured them together. A collection of beautiful objects for her enjoyment. She now realized sharply that people *lived* here: were born here, played here as children, slept and ate here. The huge scale she and Meyer delightedly wondered at was nothing to them. They drank and talked about horses and made jokes about their cocks just as comfortably here as they did in her cozy parlor.

She had never felt quite so keenly how the cozy shabbiness and the cheap wine must be part of Number Eighteen's charm. Something to laugh privately at even while you enjoyed it.

"No, thank you," she told Simon for the twentieth time as he tried to fill her plate with things she couldn't eat.

He lowered his voice, frowning. "Are you well? The journey, perhaps..."

Infatuations were a dreadful thing that turned a girl's brain to porridge. Even though she was feeling annoyed with him for bringing her here and (at this particular moment) holding a pie that reeked of oysters under her nose, she was touched by his concern. "I'm fine. I don't eat shellfish."

"Oh." He picked up the French beans in cream.

"And I'm not eating milk or cheese tonight."

He blinked. "Why not?"

She sighed. *This* conversation. "I'm Jewish. I don't eat milk and meat together, and tonight I'm eating meat."

Miss Abrami, across the table, rolled her eyes. *She* was eating whatever she liked, and to all appearances having a lovely time talking to a gentleman with the improbable name of Skeffington and the biggest ears Maggie had ever seen.

Maggie narrowed her eyes at Simon. If he said anything the slightest bit derisive—

"I didn't realize you were so...devout." Not derisive *exactly.* Dubious, maybe.

"I'm not. If I were really devout I couldn't even eat off these plates. I just—I'm Jewish." She didn't know how to explain. "That matters to me. My...I'm from Portugal."

"I know."

"Did you *know* my grandmother's father was burned at the stake for being a Jew when she was twelve years old?" She spoke more sharply than she'd meant to, angry because he was her only ally here, and he didn't understand at all.

"No," he said, plainly shocked. Was it her imagination that he was a little bemused too, that she'd raise the subject at dinner? "I'm very sorry to hear it."

"So was she, I'm sure. My family in Portugal couldn't publicly keep our laws. But we are in England, are we not?"

He nodded.

"Then I'll eat whatever I like." She was flushed and flustered, and wishing she hadn't said anything, and at the same time there was so much more she *wanted* to say.

"My mother was Jewish," Skeffington offered. "She says you can't eat leavened bread during Holy Week, either."

Maggie's heart pounded. If Skeffington's mother *had been* Jewish, she must have converted on her marriage. Been baptized so as to be properly English and have properly English children. Maggie's grandmother and great-grandmother had been baptized too, become Catholics, turned their backs on their people—but they'd have gone to the stake otherwise. That was different, wasn't it? It was all right to feel this furious at Mrs. Skeffington?

She tried to smile, brush the moment off. "That must be where you get that lovely nose from."

There was laughter around the table. Skeffington sheepishly fingered his large nose. "This hideous thing? I suppose so. It looks better on a woman, doesn't it?"

Maggie fisted her napkin in her lap. She shouldn't have come. She wished Meyer were here to say something rude. She glanced at Miss Abrami, who rolled her eyes again, but Maggie thought it was at Skeffington this time.

Lord Throckmorton leaned across Simon to ask, "But Radcliffe-Gould's uncircumcised cock doesn't violate your laws?" He didn't say it unkindly, exactly. He said it like any other harmless witticism, with a cheerful laugh and a glance at his friends. If Maggie hadn't already been on edge, she might have thought it was funny herself. God knew she and Meyer had made the same joke a hundred times, generally with a reference to sausage.

But Simon stiffened beside her. "Shut up, Clement. Shut up, all of you, and let her eat." He turned to her, and infatuation made it so the rest of the room fell away when she met his eyes. "What are the rules?"

"No shellfish," she said as quietly as she could. "No dairy tonight."

"The roast beef you're eating was probably rubbed with butter," Lord Throckmorton helpfully pointed out. "Or lard."

Maggie felt like crying. She had to eat *something*.

"Ignore him," Simon said. "Everyone else does."

Throckmorton did *not* think that was funny.

"No pork," she went on. "No rabbit. That's—that's all, I

think? I'm not very devout."

He nodded and looked over the table seriously.

She followed his eyes. Cream, butter, cheese, and more cream. "I'm sorry. I should have eaten dairy. I'll be all right with what's on my plate."

"Oy, Palliser, pass the calf's-foot jelly," Simon called across the table. "And some of those beetroots, Geoff."

The beetroots tasted mostly of pepper and burned her mouth, but she ate them all and smiled at him. He smiled back and turned the subject by launching into a rambling, rather awkward explanation of the process of designing a Gothic folly, and Maggie thought she might be a little bit in love with him.

She thought again of Skeffington's mother, who had given up her people and her history and let her children dissolve into the sea of proper *ingleses* so she could sit at a grand table like this for every meal and not feel so foreign while she did it. Or had she done it for love? Either way, Maggie couldn't even imagine wanting that. *I'm going to marry a Jew,* she promised herself. *My children will grow up knowing exactly where they belong, and being proud of it.*

That didn't mean she couldn't enjoy being a little in love with Simon Radcliffe-Gould for a while, though. He looked terribly handsome in a dark coat and white everything else, crisp as if he'd been cut out with a diamond. "...We'll begin tomorrow by walking the property in search of a likely location, and—"

"Simon, you can't wander about sketching tomorrow," said Lord Throckmorton, who had been rhapsodizing about Simon's previous brilliant designs to his other seat neighbor, a blond man of about forty who didn't look very interested. "I've arranged a treasure hunt."

This was why Simon had brought her. To protect him from this. Maggie took his arm, giving him her warmest, happiest smile. "I think we'll find some way to amuse ourselves."

He blinked uncomfortably.

"Come on, Simon, give me one day before you start working," Throckmorton said. "You deserve a holiday. Besides, some of the clues won't make sense without you."

Simon seemed to gird himself for deceit, swallowing and squaring his shoulders. But when he smiled back at Maggie, it was very convincing, bright and boyish. "If I grow bored, I'll just sketch something other than towers and ruins," he said, his voice rather husky.

There was a chorus of crowing laughter around the table, and Lord Throckmorton subsided unhappily. His blond companion looked amused.

Maggie's face burned. It was only a lie, or a joke, or something in between. But if Simon asked her to strip naked in the middle of the park so he could sketch her, Heaven help her she would do it. "I've never been an artist's model before."

Simon laughed. "You were born for it."

Maggie wasn't sure, but he might even have meant it as a compliment.

Maggie couldn't sleep. She kept going over the conversation at dinner about her eating habits and thinking of wittily acerbic things she could have said, and Simon was in bed next to her smelling absolutely delicious. It felt terribly intimate to know he smelled of port from his after-dinner drink, cedar from the traveling trunk that had held his nightshirt, a whiff of cloves and myrrh from his tooth-powder. It brought to mind a line from a Hebrew love song Meyer had taught her, that he'd translated: *Who is that coming out of the wilderness smelling of myrrh and frankincense?*

She had thrilled to learn the words, imagining an Israelite king riding out of the desert in a swirl of sand to claim his beloved. But Simon sleeping with his mouth open, yesterday's pomade sticking his black hair up haphazardly from his head, with absolutely no desire to claim her, was somehow every bit as mysterious and enthralling.

It had been days since she'd bedded anyone. She was ripe and ready for it; her breasts tingled, and she was agonizingly aware of her nightdress riding up to expose her cunny to the bedsheets. He could take her at once if he'd a mind to, push her face-down into the mattress and spear her without even having to push aside her skirts. Her thighs rubbed together when she rolled restlessly onto her other side, very nearly catching her womanly folds between them but not actually doing so.

If she could spend, it would calm her enough to sleep. But she'd promised to spend the night in his room. Would it wake him if she frigged herself? Probably, and then they'd both be embarrassed and he'd feel justly put upon. *Your appetites are unhealthy,* he'd say, or *That's revolting,* and…

…she wouldn't be able to stop, because it felt too good. She'd desperately chase her pleasure, writhing, while he watched in disgust as if she were a spider who'd crawled into his bed…

She rolled onto her back and stared at the ceiling. This

could not go on. Pushing the counterpane back, she eased herself out of bed and tiptoed across the floor.

Simon opened his eyes to see Maggie wrapping herself in her banyan and creeping to the dressing room, presumably to use the chamber pot. She eased the door closed behind her, not quite all the way so the latch wouldn't click and wake him. He turned over and tried not to be woken.

But the almost-closed door must have slipped open, because all at once he heard panting, the faint creaking of a chair, and—damn it all to hell—a low, bitten-off moan.

Simon gritted his teeth. He'd asked her not to leave his room at night, so she was trysting with someone in the damned dressing room where he could hear them? Of all the things he'd been glad to leave behind at university, having to listen to other people copulating was at the top of the list. He remembered plenty of nights with a pillow over his head, trying to decide if Clement was that vocally enthusiastic with him too, or if he was moaning loudly on purpose to make Simon jealous.

He was an adult now, and so were Maggie and whoever she was entertaining. He wasn't obliged to suffer in silence. Throwing back the covers, he stalked through the door, saying in a furious undertone, "For God's sake, you couldn't go *one night* without—"

She yanked her great tent of a dressing gown over herself, sitting bolt upright with such force that the winged chair squeaked and thumped against the wall. But Simon could not unsee what the moonlight had revealed: Maggie with one leg hooked debauchedly over the arm of her chair, a hand working furiously between her legs while the other toyed with the breast that must still be naked beneath the silk of her banyan.

It had been a perfect breast, soft and round, with a taut little nipple she'd been tugging on. Simon wanted to get his teeth on it and bite. He wanted to shove her back into that chair and make her sorry for her lack of manners, and her shapely legs, and her damn yards of gold brocade that hid them from him.

She giggled. "*Ai meu Deus*, I'm so sorry, I—" Another breathless giggle. "I thought you wouldn't hear me. I couldn't sleep, I didn't mean to be rude. I really could not sleep, and I just thought—I'm so sorry. I'll, er—" She moaned again, this time with comical disappointment. "Damnation, I was so close."

He wasn't going to be able to sleep now either. For a mad moment he thought about saying, *Carry on, I'll just be in bed doing the same.* But that was depraved, and an intimacy, and if he did it, in another few nights he'd be fucking her, 'just so we can sleep.'

"Tomorrow night I'll retire half an hour after you. Will that suffice?" Of course, that didn't solve *his* problem. But he would just have to manage.

"I think fifteen minutes would suffice," she said, nervously amused. "I wouldn't want to inconvenience you." She stood up and went back into their room. He shivered when the hem of her robe brushed his feet.

Despite her midnight embarrassment, breakfast went easier than dinner. Maggie drank chocolate, ate buttered toast with a variety of excellent preserves, and chatted with Miss O'Leary about her professional ambitions. In payment for the young woman's attendance at his party, Lord Throckmorton was leasing her a box at the Opera for the coming season, which she hoped to use to attract a better class of customers. By the time Maggie's third slice of toast had been consumed, she had invited Miss O'Leary to visit Number Eighteen, and received an open invitation to view the Opera from her box. Excellent professional opportunities for both of them.

"You, too, Mr. Radcliffe-Gould," Miss O'Leary said with a sunny smile. She wasn't a beauty in the ordinary sense, having nearly invisible eyebrows, crooked teeth, and more freckles than face, but she'd never lack for admirers. She was one of those girls you liked instinctively, for no particular reason, and she had a splendidly husky, lilting voice. "If you like the Opera."

To Maggie's surprise, Simon grinned at Lord Throckmorton. "I don't know, Clement, do I like the Opera?"

"Simon *adores* the Opera," the viscount informed them. She didn't find him any too handsome either—ruddily English, with rather protuberant pale blue eyes and sandy hair swept back from a high forehead. Nor did she find him especially charming, although perhaps in other circumstances she would have. But he was undeniably the center of the gathering. "How many times did we go to see *The Barber of Seville* this spring?"

Simon's grin turned sheepish. "...Ten?"

"A conservative estimate," Throckmorton said, launching promptly into a song in Italian. Simon glanced round the table in embarrassment and, again to her surprise, hesitantly joined in. His gruff tenor was not stage-ready, but it charmed her to death, and he did indeed know every note of the aria by heart.

He leaned forward, eyes alight and fixed on Throckmorton, and Maggie saw suddenly that however frustrated he might be with his friend now, once they had been a couple that could draw all eyes when they walked into a room. In fact, they were drawing all eyes now. Most of Throckmorton's friends looked jealous to one degree or another. She knew how they felt; *this spring* was more recent closeness than she had expected. "Do you remember when you drove us to town for every performance of Catalani in *La Clemenza di Tito*?" Simon asked.

"Not quite every one."

Simon laughed. "Yes, yes, I know, I insisted we actually study the night before our Latin exam."

"You could have studied in the curricle," Throckmorton said with mock indignation.

Suddenly Maggie missed Meyer so much it hurt. She missed how confident and safe she felt with him, how when they spoke, she felt as if she glittered and glowed, as if everyone in the room must envy their laughter. Throckmorton might be an overbearing egoist, but she didn't blame Simon for not wanting to let that feeling go.

She looked down at her beloved chemise dress, with its ruffled bodice and broad rose-colored ribbons at the sleeves and waist. She remembered finding it in a sack of clothes Mr. Gobetz brought from a widow's estate: how delighted she'd been by the little ties at the back, how she'd made Meyer do them up at once. In London, she looked splendid in it. Here, on her own, she felt foolish and a little overdressed.

What would she do if Meyer didn't come back from Rotterdam? And was she so afraid of it because he was her friend and she loved him, or because she didn't know who she was without him?

Simon stood. "Shall we tour the grounds, Miss da Silva?"

"I'd love to. Let me fetch my things."

"But we're going to play charades on the terrace," Throckmorton protested. "You love charades."

Simon looked hunted. "I know, but I really ought to get started on your Gothic ruin. You do want a Gothic ruin, don't you?"

"Yes, but I want your company too. Just stay for an hour or two, until we begin our treasure hunt. Surely that won't make any difference."

"I suppose not, but I'd like to see how the gardens look at different times of the day."

"You'll start early tomorrow."

"Miss da Silva didn't sleep well last night," Simon said, and blushed furiously. Maggie's pulse quickened. "I promised her we would take it easy today."

Throckmorton widened his eyes in a playful pout. "Please, Simon," he said in not much of an undertone. "Darling is ignoring me and I want to make him jealous." That was the older blond clergyman he'd sat with at dinner and who hadn't yet come down to breakfast, she thought. Simon's lips thinned.

Santo Deus! Throckmorton wouldn't take a hint, and Simon wouldn't do more than hint. Maggie stood up. "Lord Throckmorton, we are going on a tour of the grounds." She held his gaze unsmilingly until he looked away, which didn't take very long.

"I only thought it would be fun," he muttered, looking hurt.

"Thank you," she said evenly. "We'll see you at dinner." She turned to the footman by the sideboard. "Would you have a luncheon made up for us to take with us, please? Simon, do you need to fetch anything from the room? Pencils or drawing paper or...something?"

He darted a wary look at the viscount and nodded. "No pork, please," he called after the footman, and escaped upstairs after her.

Simon shoved a notebook and pencils into his satchel, feeling like an idiot.

Maggie was putting her own things into a pointy, tasseled purple reticule. "I begin to see why you wanted me to come with you," she said.

He felt worse. "It's contemptible, I know. I'm a man grown and I can't extricate myself from a room."

She took up a fringed parasol of sea-green silk, folded so as to dangle easily from her hand. She was all of a piece, everything matching; she knew so clearly who she was, while he knocked about from place to place like a billiard ball. A vivid memory of jeering murmurs, the brush of her curl against his shoulder, and his helpless erection filled his senses like the scent of tuberoses.

"But you knew that already," he said with an ill grace. "Or I'd never have let Henney deal that faro game."

Her expression changed from pity to annoyance. "You asked me to come."

"I know." He slung his satchel over his shoulder. "I'm sorry. Let's get out of here."

He felt a little better with sunlight and a breeze on his face. "I'm sorry," he said again, more earnestly. "None of this is your fault."

"I could teach you to say no, if you liked," she offered diffidently, and stared out across Clement's lawn as if ready to let him pretend she hadn't said anything.

"I...beg pardon?"

"There's a trick to it. I could teach you."

It was patently absurd, but his chest swelled with hope like a fringed parasol catching the wind. "All right," he said, quashing his embarrassment and preparing to learn.

They were passing a greenhouse with a sharply tilting roof, doors open to let in the summer air. As she led him inside, he removed his hat to keep clusters of unripe grapes from knocking it off. The light was dappled, green, almost murky. In her ruffled white dress she looked like Venus rising from a seafoam of embroidered handkerchiefs.

"May I touch on...sensual matters?" she asked.

Heaven help him, he nodded.

"You've gathered I enjoy...rough treatment." She seemed to be picking her words carefully, to avoid embarrassing him.

"For God's sake. You *can* speak plainly. I'm hardly a blushing virgin."

"Well, you *are* blushing." Her eyes sparkled with amusement, the light turning them very green. Instead of feeling stung by her mockery, it charmed him.

"It's a warm day," he said primly, just to see her smile widen.

"Very well then," she said. "I like men to be unkind to me in bed, and generally they know it. So sometimes when I say no, it's a game. But sometimes it isn't, and I need them to know the difference. So imagine I say to—Meyer." She faltered, and he realized she'd almost said *say to you.* "Imagine I say to him, 'No, no, oh God, please don't!'"

She said it breathily, shrinking back with a note of panic in her voice. He imagined it, holding her against the brick wall of the greenhouse as she struggled insincerely. His cock twitched in his small-clothes.

"Maybe I mean it, but maybe it's only part of the game. But now imagine I say—" She put out a hand and met his eyes squarely, her face unyielding. "Stop it. I mean it, I don't like that and I want you to stop it *right now.*" Her voice had no give to it.

He hadn't done a thing, but he took a step back.

She smiled at him. "See? How did you feel?"

"Abashed," he admitted.

She beamed. "There you go! Of course it isn't magic, but a well-meaning person would have difficulty misunderstanding. And here's the trick: for that moment, you've got to not care even a shred what they think or how they feel. You don't care if you sound like a shrew, or if they're angry with you, or even if they hate you. Believe me, they can feel it, just as you did. It's like a bucket of cold water over the head. And most people want to avoid feeling that way again. You saw Lord Throckmorton earlier. Of course he ought to have listened to you at once. But probably he told himself you really wished for an excuse to stay and enjoy yourself, that you didn't mean it, that you only wanted a little persuasion. The best way to counter that is to remove any ambiguity."

Simon thought of all the times he'd given in to Clement's persuasions. All the times he'd pretended to enjoy himself, and all the times he really had. It struck him that he likely would have remained a virgin for several more years if Clement hadn't talked over his shame and his shyness. With a sudden hot flush of guilt, he remembered how he'd silently begged Clement to ignore his protests then. Maybe Clement did believe Simon just needed an excuse to be happy.

He thought of Clement's hurt earlier at Maggie's utter indifference. Half his heart went out to Clement—and half felt glad. The truth was, Simon had a cruel streak; he had always tried not to give in to it. "I don't know if I can do that."

She shrugged. "I didn't say it was easy."

He slumped against the wall. "I've hurt him so much already. At school...I was mad for him. I still am, honestly, even if sometimes it feels more like a habit than anything else. But then...I thought I could make him happy. I wanted so badly to be the person that made him happy. I thought if I loved him enough, if I was loyal enough, he'd stop being jealous, and stop being lonely, and stop needing to be the cynosure of all eyes. And then all at once I couldn't breathe, and when I tried to say so, to explain that— He was jealous of *Catalani,* for Christ's sake. I was never any nearer her than Clement's box! But talking to him about it only made it worse. I don't know what I could have done."

She looked sorry, but—a little cynical too, as if the sad ending sounded inevitable to her, and that gave him the courage to confess the worst of it.

"But what I did do, was wait until our last day at Oxford

and tell him that I wouldn't be taking rooms with him in London like we'd planned, and I wouldn't be sleeping with him anymore, and I wouldn't be spending the rest of my life with him. And then I disappeared to go design a folly in Cornwall."

"I'm surprised he didn't follow you," she said neutrally.

"He did." Simon felt worn out. "But I went—" He could barely admit it, it was so awful. "I even went with him to buy a carpet for those imaginary rooms in London, and I knew all the while that I was leaving. Clement's been awfully forgiving. I just wish I could be more forgiving back."

"If you don't say no with your mouth, you end up saying it with your heart." She pressed her fingers tiredly into one eye. "Sometimes Meyer...don't repeat this. To anyone."

"On my honor."

Her lips twitched a little at that. He supposed poor people didn't swear on their honor. "Sometimes we have a conversation and I think, *I haven't done anything but make encouraging murmurs for the last hour and you haven't noticed.* He comes home and I say *How are you?* and he tells me and forgets to ask me back." She turned away, her Puritan straw hat hiding her face so all he could see was her mouth. "I know if I talked, he would listen. If I told him how I felt, he'd care. But I want him to ask me. And when he doesn't, I can't think of anything I want to say after all. Sometimes I think the heart is a small angry child."

His first thought was *I would notice. I would ask you how you were.* Dangerous, stupid. A bead of sweat rolled down her neck and nestled in her collarbone. All at once Clement was the farthest thing from his mind, and he didn't feel worn out at all. He felt roaringly awake. The vines smelled like summer.

She would smell like summer if he—

She sighed. "And here I am keeping you from your work after all. What sort of site is appropriate for a Gothic ruin?"

Simon had paid very little attention to Maggie for the last hour, pausing in his sketches of this or that prospect only to ask if she was *very* bored, and receive assurances that she was not. Fortunately she really wasn't, having borrowed Mrs. Edgeworth's *Castle Rackrent* from the Throckmorton library in anticipation of this very situation. It had been highly recommended to her notice by several gentlemen at Number Eighteen, none of whom had thought to mention that Sir Kit forced his young Jewish wife to eat bacon and locked her in her room for seven years. Maggie was reading along, heart in her throat, when Simon asked, "What do you think?"

She stuck a finger reluctantly in her book and closed it. "Of what?"

"Of this prospect for a ruin. There." They had paused several minutes ago on a curving path along a lake, bordered on the lakeshore by grass and on the other side by a rather comical line of small round bushes. Simon pointed out a clearing on the far shore, backed by trees. "Clement loves this lake. Of course you wouldn't be able to see it from every direction, but it would be visible all along this shore and the approach would be beautiful, if I could contrive a shape pleasing through a hundred and eighty degrees."

Maggie tried to think of other ornamental gardens she had seen. "Will it reflect in the water?"

"That's the idea." He beamed, very happy and handsome. "I shall have to make it white stone or red brick, to achieve the best effect."

"Wouldn't it be odd for medieval folks to have fronted a large building quite so close to the lake, though? Does that matter?"

He shrugged. "My father might think so—he's an antiquarian—but I don't. It isn't intended to fool people, only to be beautiful. No Greeks built temples in England either, and that doesn't stop anyone. This lake wasn't even here in medieval times. Clement's grandfather put it in."

She blinked, though she ought to have guessed it. Somehow every fresh proof of just *how* wide the gulf yawned between Maggie and the men who frequented her club was as incredible as the first. "Do you have any false lakes at your childhood home?"

He laughed. That struck her afresh, too, how darling his laugh was: a gravelly tenor *heh heh heh*. It wasn't fair! "There were a few in the neighborhood, but my father is the rector of Wath-upon-Dearne in South Yorkshire. I would guess Clement to be the richest of us, and me the poorest."

An Anglican minister. "Is he very pious?" Why should it make her uneasy to think it would break his family's heart if he married her? She had never imagined herself his wife, meeting his family. She had wanted one night, and got a fortnight of petty humiliations devoid of pleasure instead.

"Not especially, no. In England the clergy is generally more of a profession than a religious calling. A great deal is arranged through the church, you know. Marriages, births, deaths, poor relief. He takes *that* very seriously. But he leaves religious fervor to the Evangelicals."

"And your mother?"

He laughed again. "God, no. She's a Deist of the old school, though all us children are under oath not to mention the fact to my father's parishioners. Don't bring up Thomas Paine to her if you want to get away within the half hour."

She was abruptly annoyed. "I don't imagine the opportunity will arise."

He looked away. "It was a figure of speech."

Silence stretched awkwardly. She wished she hadn't been so churlish; she had no desire to introduce him to *her* mother, either.

"I'll come back tomorrow with watercolors," he said at last, leading them back toward the house. "A sketch every four hours, I should think, from sunrise to sunset." He frowned. "It will be awfully dull for you. If you'd rather spend the day with the others..."

She considered it. A day of games, society, and probably appeasing her lust with one or more of Throckmorton's guests, or a day of watching Simon paint watercolors of the same spot over and over.

There was something terribly and inexplicably attractive about that idea.

"I'll sleep through sunrise, I think," she said. "And perhaps the one after that. But you may count on me for luncheon and thereafter. I'll borrow a few more novels."

His pleased expression warmed her.

They came within sight of the house. Throckmorton perched on the terrace balustrade making notes in a little book. Managing his treasure hunt, no doubt. He raised his hand in eager greeting when he saw Simon.

A wild, possessive impulse seized her. The viscount was snide and a bother and Simon didn't belong to him, whatever Throckmorton thought. She caught at Simon's arm as he raised it in answer. "Maybe we should kiss," she said in a rush. "Just once, for show, to cement the pretense."

"Right," he answered slowly. "Of course. As we talked about in the carriage."

"Exactly."

He gave a jerky little nod.

She took hold of his lapels and kissed him.

Chapter 4

S imon stood rigidly straight, kissing her back with only a slight stirring of his lips, but his chest rose and fell sharply against her knuckles. So Maggie curled a hand around the back of his neck and touched her mouth to his again, hope wriggling in her stomach like a fish.

His mouth opened beneath hers with a gasp, his arms curving around her shoulders. His splayed fingers lifted her against him gently, making her throat close as if she'd swallowed honey. Sweetness pooled between her legs and sparkled like sugar in her chest. Their tongues met; he tasted like the wine in the picnic basket currently dangling from his hand and knocking against her knees.

When she pulled back, his fingers tightened—but he said ruefully, "I think we shouldn't do that again. I liked it too much."

She smiled at his dazed expression, feeling sad and triumphant at once. "Let me know if you change your mind."

His bark of laughter was startled, appalled, or maybe just strangled. But he tangled his fingers with hers as they went back toward the house, swinging their hands between them. It might have been for Throckmorton's benefit, but it felt friendly.

The quiet of the lakeshore at dawn, the grass wet with dew and the first rays of sunlight gilding the cool lake, had convinced Simon his choice of location was a right one. He was filled with tired, confident peace: a rare and highly enjoyable occurrence. A couple hours more of sleep before his eight o'clock drawing would be just the thing.

His watercolor had dried on his way back to the house. Holding it by one corner, he slipped his boots off in the corridor and entered the bedroom in his stocking feet, smothering a yawn. The curtains were drawn, but enough light filtered in to faintly illuminate the bed.

He stopped, as if he had opened the door onto a stiff wind.

Maggie's face was half-buried in the pillow and a lumpy heap of counterpane covered most of her, but her arms were stretched out toward his empty side of the bed. One bare leg emerged from beneath the quilt. Her cap had slipped in the night, and a slice of dark hair and two long rag-ends peeked out. When he had come in last night, fifteen minutes after she retired, she'd been dampening her hair at the basin, rolling it into curls, and tying it up with strips of rag.

Somehow it was so much harder to resist her in the dim light of morning, with this sleepy quiet in his heart. Or—not to *resist* her, for she was only sleeping, and offered no arguments or seduction. But his own attraction to her drifted up and he couldn't find the energy to quash it. If she woke now and smiled, he would go to her.

Yesterday's kiss still rattled around inside him like a marble in an empty box.

He stripped to his shirt and pantaloons and climbed into bed. Her outflung hands were inches from his face; he could smell her juices on them.

Her eyes opened when his weight settled on the mattress, but she squeezed them shut again and turned her face into the pillow, curling inward.

His disappointment was crushing.

"Mona," Clement said diffidently. There was no one else at breakfast, though it was past ten. Simon supposed everyone had been up late, and probably drunk their own weight in brandy besides. Clement himself was pale, his eyes bloodshot and his movements careful.

Simon's heart clenched. *You should take better care of yourself.* But if Clement ever did, it would be in his own time. Simon's efforts had only ever served to annoy him.

"Yes, Clementine?" he said, using the old pet name since they were alone.

"I have to call on my mother this morning. Would you come with me?"

Oh, God. "Of course." Simon got up to pour himself another cup of coffee for the ordeal ahead. "How did you get her to remove to the Dower House, anyway?"

"She hasn't," Clement said glumly. "She's still living in her old rooms here. She's only staying there for the party, and *that* took me a week to talk her into."

Simon shuddered in sympathy. Clement's mother loved

him dearly—at least, Simon thought she did—but she was not easy to be around, and her idea of maternal behavior was unorthodox, to say the least.

"She's got a dog now," Clement said, even more glumly. "It's horrible. Don't say I didn't warn you."

The King Charles spaniel had a whining face even for a spaniel, but Simon wouldn't have held that against her if not for the barking, which was singularly piercing, excited, and unremitting. Lady Throckmorton beamed. "Look, Hetty likes you!" Hetty bounded onto the settee, climbed into Simon's lap, and began leaping for his face, still barking. "How have you been?"

"Well, thank you." Simon extended his neck as far as it would go.

"Leave Simon alone," Clement told the dog, lifting her back to the ground. She climbed back up, undeterred.

"Oh, Simon doesn't mind, do you? Do you need anything in the village, Simon? I've been meaning to take my phaeton out. I think the fresh air would do me good and Hetty loves driving. Don't you, Hetty?"

Simon's relief when she plucked the dog out of his lap and into her own warred with his terror at the idea of getting into her phaeton. Lady Throckmorton was not an unskilled driver, but an inattentive and fearless one, prone to sudden stops that threatened, in an open phaeton, to send one flying over the horses' heads. After years of silent terror, Simon had finally vowed never again to let her drive him after a particularly harrowing journey when she hadn't looked at the road for more than five seconds together, being occupied in asking him questions about his personal life and showing him the miniature of himself Clement had given her for her birthday.

"Should you like to go for a drive?" she crooned to the dog, which licked her face and bucked about in her hands. "I think she would!"

Clement made an apologetic face at Simon. "We wouldn't all fit in your phaeton, Mama."

"Oh, we could squeeze in."

"Hetty's barking will fright the horses. They almost ran away with us last time."

Simon blanched.

"They've grown accustomed to her by now," Lady Throckmorton said blithely, rising from her seat. Clement and Simon stood—out of politeness, but it looked like assent. "Let me fetch my pelisse."

Simon thought of Maggie's training in saying no. He stifled a giggle, imagining using such blunt tactics on Clement's mother.

But why not? Would he really risk his neck to preserve his manners, when Lady Throckmorton had so few of her own? "My lady." She ignored him. He repeated himself, louder.

"Yes, Simon, what is it?"

"I'm sorry, but I'd rather not go."

"Oh, don't be silly, you could use the fresh air too. I'm sure you boys have been burning the candle at both ends."

"Lady Throckmorton." He waited until she raised her eyes, and then, despite his inner quailing, looked her coolly in the face. *I don't care what she thinks. I don't care if she's angry. I don't care if she thinks my manners are atrocious.* "I don't want to go. Let's say no more about it."

The words dropped like stones into the—well, it wasn't silence, for Hetty was still yipping.

"Oh!" Lady Throckmorton sat with a nervous laugh. "If you feel *that* strongly about it, I'll go alone, later. But surely you need something in the village. To mail a letter perhaps."

Simon felt terrible. He shook his head.

She fussed with her skirts, not looking at him. "How have you been? It's been so long since you visited."

He swallowed a protest that it hadn't been *that* long. "I'm well, thank you. I've just been in town." He hardly dared glance at Clement—but his friend mimed an admiring whistle. Simon flushed with sudden, sheepish triumph. It had worked! He didn't have to go driving with Lady Throckmorton!

"Would you like some more tea, then?"

Simon was already buzzing from all the coffee he'd drunk at breakfast, but he thought it behooved him to be gracious in victory. "That would be lovely, thank you."

"Sugar, no milk?"

"Milk and extra sugar, please."

"Oh, have you changed it? It always used to be no milk."

It had been milk and extra sugar for as long as Simon had been drinking tea, but he nodded. "My sweet tooth grows every year, I'm afraid. May I have another macaroon as well? They're delicious."

She patted her cap. "I let you boys have the house, but I brought Cook with me."

"Clever of you."

"It's actually rather refreshing, living alone. Consulting no one's wishes but my own."

Simon tried to remember an instance when she had consulted anyone else's.

"I've been thinking of taking a lover," she confided with a giggle. "Do you think Mr. Fleming would be discreet?"

Clement's look of horror went to Simon's heart. "Father's lawyer? Mama, Father's only been dead three months."

"You needn't look at me like I'm Queen Gertrude! I don't mean to *marry* Mr. Fleming. But celibacy leads to all kinds of nervous disorders and health troubles, you know." She winked at Simon, who tried not to cringe. "Honestly, Clement, I only think of it because I miss your father so terribly."

Clement, recovering his equilibrium, did no more than roll his eyes in Simon's direction. "I miss him too."

"But how are you, Simon?"

"I'm well," Simon told her again. "I'm still designing ornamental garden buildings. I've done one this year already, for Lord Pendleton, and I'm doing one for Clement now."

She clapped her hands together. "Of course you are! My my, a man of business. You were always such a hardworking, ambitious boy. I knew you would be a great success at something or other. Why weren't you more like Simon, Clement?" She sighed. "I suppose it was my fault, wasn't it? How did your parents make you so well-behaved, Simon?"

Simon wished he could sink into the floor. This was not the first time, or even the twentieth time, that Lady Throckmorton had told Clement he ought to be more like Simon. But it never became less upsetting—for Clement either, he presumed, though they had never discussed it, choosing instead to pass it over in awkward silence.

"Are you thinking of marrying, Simon?" the viscountess went on.

Simon felt something very like panic. He had frequently considered, if he did one day want to marry, how painful it would be to inform Clement of the fact. He should have agreed to the drive; he might have broken his neck but at least they wouldn't be having this conversation.

"I'm sure your mother must long to see you settled. I want grandbabies myself, you know, but Clement doesn't care about *that*. He wouldn't even consent to be introduced to Miss Duckworth-Trevelyan last Season. Don't you think Miss Duckworth-Trevelyan is a charming girl who would suit him admirably?"

"I don't believe I have the pleasure of her acquaintance."

"Simon isn't going to marry any time soon," Clement said, very pale. "Seeing as he brought a little Jewish trollop to my house party."

Despite the brief shock of hurt and betrayal, Simon still felt sorry enough for his friend that his "Clement, don't," lacked conviction.

It spurred Clement on anyway. "A charming girl, Mama, and in *no* danger of any nervous disorders."

Lady Throckmorton blinked. "A Jewess! Oh Simon. Are you sure that's wise? I know some men find their women very pretty, with those dark mysterious eyes, but you know they hate us really. How can you ever sleep easy next to one?"

Clement laughed, looking at Simon as if to say, *Good Lord, where does she get this stuff from?*

Simon did not know what to say. It was pointless and improper to say anything, and yet how would he look Maggie in the face, later, if he said nothing?

If he did marry her, Lady Throckmorton would expect to be *introduced* to her, and God only knew what she would say then!

He shook his head. Where had that come from? Of course he had no thought of marrying her. "I won't defend Miss da Silva to you," he said at last, "because it would imply her worth is a matter for debate. I will only say that at the moment, I esteem her higher than either of you."

Indeed, why was he here at all? He looked at the pair of them, and suddenly he understood what Maggie had meant. Just now, he did not care a shred what they thought or felt. What difference did it make if they were angry with him?

He had sat still and been polite to Clement's mother for years, with no reward he could see, except that she thought his manners prettier than Clement's. If he walked out now, would she even remember it next time he saw her? And was there any reason, at this late date, to believe that Clement would reward Simon's restraint with restraint of his own?

Simon stood. "Thank you very much for the macaroons, my lady. I bid you good morning." He bowed and walked out.

Clement didn't follow him, which set his stomach churning by habit. It would be days of silent treatment for this.

What if Clement dropped him for good and all? What if he finally realized Simon would never change his mind, and so there was nothing to be gained from bothering with him any longer? Who would Simon write to, if Clement dropped him? Who would he tell about books, and sheet music, and funny things girls said to him in shops?

He ignored the fear, setting off for the main house. But it

was only a minute or two before Clement called out behind him, "Oy, Simon!"

He waited, startled. He had been so sure it would be silent treatment. Had he judged Clement of six-and-twenty by the behavior of Clement as a student?

"I'm sorry," Clement said. "I was only trying to get a rise out of my mother."

Simon could pretend to believe that, or he could say what he thought and likely be told he was being fanciful, and doubt himself. He was so tempted to be grateful for the apology, and let it go.

Maggie wouldn't let it go. Simon decided to risk it. "I think you wanted to get a rise out of me too. But it isn't my fault your mother said something unkind, and it isn't Miss da Silva's either." He hesitated. "And I'm tired of your jealousy and spite," he concluded in a rush. "I want nothing more than to stay friends, but you make it damned difficult sometimes."

Clement flinched back as if Simon had struck him. "Spite? Is that what you think of me? That I'm some cattish old woman?"

Was he being unjust? Simon felt the worst sort of heel, but he could not seem to dig up any more patience and charity inside himself. "After all these years I suppose I know better than to expect honesty from you. But we both know you've done your best to make Miss da Silva feel unwelcome. And don't give me the silent treatment, either!" he said as Clement's face froze and he began to turn away. "Tell me the truth."

"It hurts to see you with her, that's all." Clement's eyes were too bright. "I don't accuse you of *spite*, but it wasn't kind of you to bring her."

"And is that why you invited Mr. Darling?" Simon demanded. "To hurt me? Or was it because he's your lover and you wanted his company?" *For some unfathomable reason,* he added silently.

Clement grinned sheepishly. "A little of both?"

Simon laughed. God, what was wrong with him? Even now, a small part of him was flattered by Clement's jealousy. Being desired always had startled and delighted him. It was so far from how he saw himself. Clement and Maggie were so brilliant and dazzling, so surrounded by admirers, and yet they chose plain old Simon.

"*Is* Aloysius hurting you?" Clement looked through his lashes.

A familiar jolt of lust hit Simon. "Of course," he admitted. He'd never liked seeing Clement with other boys. It wasn't even that he'd wanted fidelity; he'd only been afraid Clement would find someone he liked better. He had half resented all of Clement's friends, and still did after everything.

Should he have talked to Clement about it? If he had, if he'd said a lot of things, if he'd said no to a lot of things years ago...would they still be lovers? Or would it have been over much sooner? "But it is what it is. I don't blame you for loving him."

"He doesn't love me." Clement put his hands in his pockets. "He went off with Skeffington yesterday, and stayed away all night. And he isn't...considerate of me. In bed, I mean."

"You should give him his marching orders." Simon didn't put much force into the words. He knew Clement wouldn't.

"I should. But you know I'm no good without"—there was a pause, and then Clement nobly did not say *without you*—"a lover. I just cry all the time. And I can't squander my time in tears at the moment. After you swarm of locusts depart, I've got to get down to business. Managing the estate and all that." He glanced at Simon out of the corner of his eyes. "Are you sure you don't want to give it another shot?"

And just like that, Simon's lungs closed. "If we give it another shot, there won't be anything left when we're done," he said, trying to soften it. "And I want there to be something left. Clementine, I know I was the one who broke it off, but don't you remember how miserable we were? We were too close. I couldn't breathe. Surely you couldn't either."

Clement chuckled unhappily. "Oh, I'm more suffocating than you are. I'll be just like my mother when I'm old, won't I? Listening to her talk is like looking upon my doom."

"Of course not!" Simon said feelingly.

"I will. I hardly have the option of being like my father. The man never opened his mouth. I suppose he saw there was no point to it. I'm sorry I dragged you with me to see her. I don't want to drive off Aloysius, and..."

And he hadn't wanted to go alone. "I know. That's all right."

"And I'll be nice to Miss da Silva. I promise."

"Thank you."

Simon had finished his noon watercolor of the lake and was trying to concentrate on sketches of designs for the folly, but Maggie was asleep again on the blanket beside him in a syllabub of skirts and a cherry-red sash, which he himself had tied in a large bow at her back that morning. Her face was buried in her arms, her hat laid atop her hair to keep off the sun. One calf in a clocked stocking protruded from her petticoats.

He was losing his mind.

The sun was uncomfortably warm; when she slept with such abandon, why shouldn't he take off his coat?

But he kept it on as the afternoon advanced and the heat worsened. Miss da Silva awoke at last, rolling onto her back. Feeling her sleeve and side where they had rested against the ground and were now soaked in sweat, she wrinkled her nose. "I need a bath. Or at least some more perfume."

Simon could smell tuberoses even now, faintly. "No more perfume."

She looked contrite. "I'm sorry, do I use too much? It's so hard to tell. I mostly stop smelling it myself after an hour or two."

"No," he said. "That isn't what I meant."

She shrugged and tilted her face up to the sun, shutting her eyes contentedly. "It hasn't been this warm in years. I think I might go for a swim."

Simon could feel his eyes turning to saucers.

"Would you like to join me?"

He shook his head.

She frowned at him. "You're wilting. You should at least take off your coat."

"I'm fine."

"I'm not a lady, you know. I wouldn't be offended by the sight of your sleeves."

"I *don't want to*."

His sharpness took her aback, but she collected herself

quickly. "All right," she said peaceably. "I'm sorry, I didn't mean to mother you."

It still startled him, the ease with which she gave in.

Her gown wrapped around and over her, pinned and tied, but she deftly removed it all, starting with the knot he'd made in her sash. Stays, stockings, and shoes rapidly followed, and into the lake she waded. "*Ai meu Deus* it's cold," she gasped. "And I meant to be good and keep my hair dry! Ah well, here goes." She ducked under, surfacing with a gasp. Simon saw her wet shift plastered to the inward dip of her waist before she dove in again.

She came up in the middle of the lake, her smile exuberantly blinding. Her shift floated around her like a jellyfish. "The water's lovely! Are you sure you don't want to come in?"

"I'm working." He wished it weren't a lie. He was doodling windows and archways, but mostly he was watching her.

She hesitated a moment, then bobbed onto her back and paddled off, her body unselfconsciously on display. The sun sparkled off the water she threw up as she went.

He didn't actually *need* to do anything until his next watercolor at three. It had been a long time since he'd gone for a swim, and he loved it. What was he afraid of? That he would be overwhelmed by desire and ravish her there in the water?

Well, that was certainly part of it.

A sudden, brutal image slammed through him: *dragging her to him as she resisted. She was thrashing to get away, but she would have to calm and submit if she didn't wish to go under. She would cling to him, permitting any liberty—* The sun beat down and his pulse raced, his face so hot he felt feverish. His cock ached sharply. It was disgusting. *He* was disgusting. Being dunked in cold water would do him good.

Why was he so intent on resisting?

He remembered what Maggie had said. *If you don't say no with your mouth, you end up saying it with your heart.* The more he looked at that truth, the more it stretched and twisted, curving back on itself like a stone serpent eating its tail on a cathedral wall.

Simon had lied and said no to a lot of things he'd wanted. Once he'd given Clement an inch, Simon had never had the strength to keep him from taking a mile—so eventually he'd started withholding the inches too. Had he forgotten how to say yes? He could barely hear his heart speaking anymore; he only remembered that he couldn't trust it. It was an organ as perverse, overeager, and contrary as his cock.

But he did know he wanted to get into that water. It didn't have to be all or nothing. He didn't have to fuck her just because he went for a swim. And, he realized with a deep sense of relief, Maggie wouldn't press him to.

He turned away as he stripped down to his shirt—he had unfortunately omitted small-clothes to preserve the line of his pantaloons—but he heard her whoop of triumph and realized he was grinning. He plunged into the water with an enthusiasm he'd forgotten, momentarily startled by how the water slowed him down and he had to struggle to walk forward. He gave up the struggle and dove under.

Maggie caught her breath when Simon came up out of the water laughing, slicking his hair out of his eyes. Wet, it was black as jet, and clung glittering to his scalp. She could almost see the color of his skin through his wet shirt. His shoulders and arms were beautiful, like something carved in marble by a sculptor who loved his model.

Lust fizzed like champagne in her throat, purely happy even though she knew she couldn't have him. She was alive and it was summer, the sun on the lake was beautiful and he was beautiful. She splashed water at him with her cupped hand and he splashed back, looking happy too, as if his fine clothes had trapped him and now he was free.

She had missed this weightless liberty so much, legs and arms flailing, water slipping and sliding against her skin, ducking under the surface and coming up for a great breath of fresh air. She wanted so much to take her shift off too and swim naked.

Simon ducked under the water and grabbed her ankle. She shrieked, accidentally kicking him in the shoulder, and they both laughed and splashed and raced each other back and forth across the lake. And even though she was flushed with wanting him, she hadn't felt so pure in a long time, so at one with the world and free of calculation or design. She ought to spend more time out-of-doors in the sun. She ought to leave the city more.

The thought ruined the innocence of the moment. Her own meaning was so transparent: Simon worked out-of-doors, and was rich enough to travel and stay at friends' palaces with grounds bigger than Hyde Park. She felt greedy, and disloyal to Meyer, who took her out of the city whenever they could afford it. How was Meyer? Was he sad right now, and missing his father? Was he missing her?

What if he wasn't missing her? What if right now he was thinking, *I ought to leave England more*?

"What's wrong?"

"I'm getting cold, that's all. I'd better go in."

Even during the hottest summer in years, it wasn't warm enough in England to let the shift dry on her body. She took it off and wrung it out, sluicing water from her skin with the flat of her hand. She didn't look to see if Simon was watching her.

Slipping her dry petticoat over her head, she spread the shift on the grass and let down her hair to dry. Then she pulled a pencil and paper from her satchel and wrote a letter to Meyer.

"Who are you writing to?"

She looked up with a start, relieved to have been focused enough on her letter that she hadn't heard him coming. But relief fled at the sight of Simon buttoning his pantaloons. She caught a glimmer of skin and a few dark curly hairs in the gaps between buttons before he pulled up the flap. And just as she dragged her eyes unwillingly upward, he pulled his sodden shirt over his head.

She tried and failed to swallow, making a sound like a beached fish. His chest was pale but beautiful, with a spray of freckles on his left shoulder above his collarbone. She could see the hair under his arms, and the smattering of dark hair in the center of his chest.

Maggie smothered a laugh at that; she and Meyer were wont to mock hairless Englishmen. But suddenly there was something raw and sweet in that unprotected expanse of chest, his dark pink nipples standing out like...

She couldn't think clearly enough to finish the sentence. She wanted with single-minded ferocity to take his nipple in her mouth. She wanted to push him back on the blanket and touch and bite and lick and kiss every inch of exposed skin while he laughed and pretended to push her away.

He spread his shirt by her shift and dropped onto the blanket. "Who are you writing to?" he asked again. The color was high in his cheeks, but his voice made a convincing show of nonchalance about their current mutual state of undress.

She made herself look at his face. That turned out to be worse, all that bare skin blurred at the edges of her vision. "Meyer. Do you think Lord Throckmorton would frank the letter for me?"

Simon blinked. "I'd forgotten, Clement can frank letters now." He smiled with grudging but unmistakable affection. "I'm sure he'd be delighted to demonstrate his new privilege."

Maggie felt a pang of jealousy. Folding up the letter, she put it in her satchel to finish later. "I'm to send it to his father's office so his mother doesn't see it." She sighed. "She's probably throwing brides at him as we speak." She could picture them, pretty demure girls with gold in their hair and ears, whose mothers had taught them to make perfect puffy *gemberboles* and say the prayers on Shabbat and probably play the pianoforte.

"Would it upset you if he married?"

"I think it would, yes." She huffed a laugh. "Even though I don't want to marry him myself. What's that expression—dog in the manger?"

"It's funny, isn't it?" He lay back on the blanket, knotting his fingers together behind his head. She wanted to lie down and listen to his heartbeat. "I knew Clement was jealous of me. He doesn't like that you're here; I dread one day having to tell him I love someone else. But until this morning, I didn't really admit that I'm jealous of him too. I hate Aloysius Darling."

"I don't think that's only jealousy. Aloysius Darling is an ass."

To her surprise, he reached up and curled a loose lock of her hair around his finger. "Where did you learn to swim?"

She held herself very still so his hand wouldn't brush her breast. If it did, he'd pull back. "In Lisbon as a little girl. And Meyer and I have gone down to Brighton a few times. He can visit the Peerless Pool in summer, but of course mere women are not allowed."

"People do swim in the Thames, I believe," he offered dubiously.

"I can see by your face you wouldn't risk swallowing that water either."

To her regret, he dropped her hair. "Do you miss Lisbon?"

"Yes, though I wouldn't want to go back. The sunlight is yellow and the water's nearly turquoise. Unless colors are always brighter in memories of childhood, I don't know. I was only six when my mother brought me here. I know the beaches in Lisbon are soft sand, not like the hard pebbles at Brighton that hurt your feet." She dug her bare toes into the grass, remembering. "I don't have many memories of my father, but I remember holding onto him in the waves and knowing he'd keep my head above the water." Absently, she brushed a bit of her hair across her mouth—and then realized she'd taken up the same tress he'd been toying with.

She flushed, hoping he hadn't noticed, and made herself keep talking. "A lot of soldiers wrote home about Portugal during the war. Everyone was talking all over town about the awful food, the garlic, the sardines...it made me dreadfully homesick. When we went to the beach, my father would buy us *sardinhas assadas* and pieces of *torrão de Alicante*."

"What's that?"

"A sweet made of almonds and egg whites. I buy it in the East End sometimes, but either they don't make it the same, or I've forgotten what it really tasted like." She looked at him. "What do they eat in Yorkshire? Other than Yorkshire pudding."

He laughed that distinctive, endearing laugh. "I admit I do love Yorkshire pudding. At home it's often a first or last course, not a remove like in the south. Our nurse used to smother it with jam and powdered sugar. I wish I had some right now."

Beads of water still shimmered in his navel and collected in the hollows of his chest, the dip at the center of his ribcage. "And around Whitsuntide, the dairy-man always tithed left-over curds for cheese tarts, another Yorkshire delicacy. When one was baking you could smell rosewater and clove-pepper— that's what we call allspice up there—all over the house. I used to beg to eat it as it came out of the oven puffed up like a cloud, but with the wisdom of age I can see it would be runny and burn my mouth..."

Eventually the sun dried them, and their clothes. Her shift billowed slightly as if to blow away every time a breeze came across the lake and ran through the grass, but neither of them made any move to dress. Somehow over an hour passed, only in describing food and sharing the food that was in their basket. They talked on while he painted the lake twice more (moving on to favorite holidays, fables, and per-formers at Astley's Amphitheater; amusing family squabbles;

and other equally vital topics).

Words poured out of them as they finally dressed, walked back to the house, and ate dinner. Maggie was conscious that they were being rude and ignoring the rest of the party, and that Lord Throckmorton looked more unhappy every time Simon laughed, despite the other guests' efforts to cheer him—but she couldn't stop talking. After dinner they escaped upstairs without port or tea and talked on their bed about nothing of consequence until nearly two in the morning, exclaiming with delight at every point of agreement or coincidence, and with almost equal delight when disagreement offered an opportunity for debate.

It was that particular species of conversation that was colored through and through by showing off, by knowing the other person thought you pretty and witty and generally splendid, and loving that he thought it because he was the best thing you'd ever seen. The kind of conversation that made you feel slightly foxed. Discovering they'd both watched the sham naval battle on the Serpentine when the Tsar was in London felt like...fate.

It was, Maggie admitted to herself, the kind of conversation you had with someone when you were about to fall in love and you just couldn't wait for it to happen.

Chapter 5

Simon had come to Throckmorton to work. He'd brought Maggie here so he could *work*. And now for the third day in a row he was accomplishing nothing, because he would rather be talking to her than doing anything else on earth. He bubbled over with things to say to her.

He sat dutifully at a library table with his books spread around him, and he'd been staring at the same illustrated plate of archways for the last twenty minutes.

He couldn't remember the last time he'd felt this way. Well, he could remember the last time he hadn't been able to concentrate on work—that happened all the time. But this happiness...

No, he *did* remember: Clement, years ago. Deep down, he'd been afraid he'd never feel this way again. That at five-and-twenty, he'd had his chance at a great love and ruined it. But that was foolish, wasn't it? He was only five-and-twenty, and England was full of people.

Just now, England seemed very full of Maggie, in the best way possible.

He looked up—raised his eyes the merest fraction—and there she was, curled up on a sofa and frowning slightly over her letter. That dip of her brow in profile was a lovely thing.

He copied it in miniature with his pencil, on his fourth try satisfied that he had done it justice. And then he was drawing her. The graceful line of her profile, the curve of her ear, the upsweep of her hair disappearing under a smooth bandeau with a few ringlets tumbling over, the slope of her neck and shoulders. He supposed by her loose posture that she wore her short stays today.

Easy familiarity with another person's underthings was an intimacy he hadn't had in a long time. Yes, his thwarted arousal at being surrounded by her scent and linens was annoying, but he had missed sharing quarters with someone other than a valet.

As he mused, his hand added the surrounding architecture without conscious direction: bas-relief wooden columns, delicate gilt ironwork on the spiral staircases and the balustrades of the second story of bookshelves, the portrait of Clement's grandmother that hung between the windows.

It was a neat little drawing, but his favorite thing in it was still that first curve of her eyebrow.

"Do you think white plaster or red brick would look better reflected in the lake?" he asked, more to start a conversation than because the question preoccupied him overmuch at the moment.

She glanced up, mouth working pensively. "I think red brick would look best at noon," she said at last, "but white would show more at all hours of the day."

"Then we're of one mind." He was inordinately pleased by their agreement, and by the aptness of her observation. "I—"

"I beg your pardon," she said apologetically, "but I want to finish this letter to my mother, and my spelling in Portuguese isn't good enough to allow for distractions."

Her tone was conciliatory, her smile charming, but his heart sank. Every part of him sank; the high ceiling appeared suddenly further away. "Turnabout is fair play," he said, striving to sound unaffected and wishing he'd kept silent instead. "You've been distracting me all morning."

She was flattered by the admission, at least. She ducked her head and bit her lip to hide her smile. "Have I really? I'm sorry, I know you brought me so you could do more work, not less. Here, I'll remove us both from the path of temptation." And gathering her things from the sofa just on the other side of his writing desk, she took herself to another at the far end of the library.

Simon tried to decide if the sun had actually gone behind a cloud, or if it was his imagination.

I'm sure he was telling himself you really wanted an excuse to enjoy yourself, she had said of Clement. It turned out that Clement was right. Simon had been working for three years now, but not...not *steadily*. He waited too long between commissions, he neglected his studies.

His father had warned him, gently, when Simon told him he meant to design follies. *Of course some of your school friends will be idle all their lives, but honorable labor does not demean a gentleman. I know it's difficult. I envied your uncle James when we were children, because he would inherit everything. But I think I got the best of it in the end.*

The implication that this wasn't real, honorable labor had made him furious at the time, but maybe he *had* chosen this profession because he had thought it would be easy, something he could do in his spare time. What if he didn't have the staying power to make a real success of it? He did resent that Clement would never have to work, and he did. He had nothing in the bank and he *could not* ask his father or Clement for a loan.

What does your mother think of your profession? he longed to ask Maggie, but she had made it clear that conversation was unwelcome.

Every ruin he put his pencil to was dull and lifeless. He spread old sketches out on the table, searching for inspiration, but there was a buzzing in his head and all he could think was, *Have I had my last good idea?*

At length Maggie approached him, perching on the edge of the writing table. Her skirts tucked themselves under her arse and then cascaded downward like a waterfall or maybe a sonnet. The desire to hook his arm round her waist and drag her in overwhelmed him. He could bury his face in her bosom and block out everything else.

She reached out and pulled his sketch toward her. "Oh, what a lovely drawing of the library. Look, you've put me in it! May I send it to my mother?"

He agreed, though he'd wanted to keep it.

She smiled and tucked it into her letter before preparing to seal it. "I'll ask Lord Throckmorton to frank them after dinner. I'm sorry I was rude earlier. Which of these designs are you considering?"

None of them. He barely kept from stuffing them all under a book to hide them from her view.

He didn't like how much he wanted to abandon his pencil and sit on the sofa and show off his books to her. He didn't like, either, that he had been waiting anxiously for her to deign to speak to him. "I haven't accomplished as much as I was hoping to this morning. You needn't wait about for me all day, if you'd rather join the others and enjoy yourself." She hadn't said a word about her frustrated desire, but he remembered she'd asked permission to disport herself with the other guests.

Once again, everyone would be having fun but him.

She drew back a little, looking disappointed. "Are you sure? You said you wanted me to keep you from being hounded from your work."

He smiled, determined for her not to see even a shadow of his resentment. "I'm sure. Maybe you can even find Clement in time for your letters to make today's post."

"All right. I like this one, by the way." She pushed one of his sketches toward him, and hopped off the table.

The drawing was an elevation of the ruined transept of Roche Abbey, near Maltby in Yorkshire. Now that the door had shut behind her, his brain sharpened. He disliked the proportions of it: a soaring ground floor where the chapel must have been, a squat center story crammed with blind arched windows (Clement had said that must be where Robin Hood and Little John hid when they came to hear Mass), and the whole topped with mid-sized round arches, out of place above their pointed brethren.

But there *was* something about how the wall zigged and zagged brokenly along, flat from the front but attracting the eye with its protrusions from the side. What if he evened out the stories and made all the windows of a size? Sky through an empty arched window was always arresting. A plain double lancet arch topped with a quatrefoil, perhaps...He flipped through Carter's *Ancient Architecture* to a plate on windows and, taking a new sheet of paper, began hastily to sketch.

Maggie shut the library door quietly behind her, trying not to feel disappointed. After all, she'd told him to hush when she wanted to concentrate; it was his prerogative to do the same. She ought to take this opportunity to slake her lust, which was growing tiresomely, with one of the other guests. They were probably outdoors, enjoying the sun. She headed upstairs to put on her boots.

On the stairs, she met...she tried to think of their names. The skinny one talked a lot and had a saint in his name, and his father had met his mother in India, and the heavyset one talked very little...Sir Joseph? "Good morning, gentlemen," she said at last, with a smile. "Have you been enjoying the party?"

They looked at one another and laughed in a way that made Maggie think maybe they had been enjoying each other. The idea was not without appeal—and they were the only members of the party other than Miss O'Leary that hadn't done anything to annoy her yet. "Throckmorton is an excellent host," Mr. Saint said. "Where's Radcliffe-Gould?"

"Oh, he's working," she said, not specifying where so as not to give them the idea of going there. "I wasn't of much use to him at the moment," she added flirtatiously.

"Beauty must always be useful to an artist," Mr. Saint said promptly. Sir Whatsit made a noise of agreement and smiled shyly at her.

It was a lovely compliment, and they both had very nice smiles. Why be subtle? "Might I be of use to you gentlemen?"

Mr. Saint's eyes lit up.

Of course the tip of Simon's pencil snapped on his second page of windows. Reaching for his penknife, he remembered he had left it in yesterday's pantaloons. He dug through the library table drawers, but the only knife was hopelessly dull. He'd have to go upstairs and fetch his own.

Moans and small cries became audible as he approached the stairs, growing in volume as he started up them. He hastened his steps, preparing to avert his eyes and feign not to hear any lewd remarks addressed to himself.

The woman made a small, sobbing noise of protest. Was that—Maggie? That hadn't taken long.

Even though Simon had known this was a possibility when he'd told her to go and enjoy herself with the others, he hadn't expected to *see* it. He weighed the added inconvenience and awkwardness of going back down and taking the servants' stair.

It wasn't worth it—and he wanted to see. He decided to brush past with a quick nod, but in the event the entire landing was blocked by Maggie and not one but two men.

Sir Geoff was quietly but intently rogering Maggie, on her hands and knees before him. St. Aubyn was trying to get at her breasts, and experiencing difficulties with her bodice. "Pick her up," he told Sir Geoff, who wrapped one powerful arm around Maggie's ribcage and hefted her so she knelt upright. She moaned as his other hand disappeared beneath her skirts.

"Oh, good morning, Radcliffe-Gould," St. Aubyn said, hands pausing on Maggie's bosom.

She hadn't realized it was him. Her head whipped toward him, and their eyes met. Simon could not pretend now that the longing he saw in them was for him to save her—or that he wanted to. He was hard as stone.

And he had seen her put on her dress this morning. "There's a drawstring below the ruffle at her neck." He came forward, trying to recall the time in his life when this sort of thing had been commonplace to him.

Only it never had been. He had always been acting a part, trying to seem confident and as if the three pairs of eyes on him didn't feel like a million.

He liked that, though. It was the only circumstance in which he did like being watched: it heightened everything, made it hotter and tinglier and more undeniable. He flipped up Maggie's ruffle and undid the small tie, as he'd wanted to that morning. She gasped, breasts lifting toward him.

He untied the drawstring at her waist, too. Her bodice gaped open to reveal her stays. He kept his voice steady, hoping they couldn't tell how his pulse was racing. "And these are tied off at the bottom." He slipped his fingers beneath her petticoat, pricking himself on a pin when Sir Geoff thrust into her. Maggie's mouth fell open.

Oh God. He wanted sex so badly. He wanted *her* so badly.

He could unbutton his breeches and slip himself into her mouth. No one would stop him, least of all her. He found the slip-knot in her stay-laces, and tugged it free. The corset relaxed, and she drew in a deep breath. Simon, in contrast, couldn't get enough air.

Naked hope was blazoned across Maggie's face; it hurt. She wanted him to touch her breasts. He could hear Sir Geoff's groin slapping against hers, splendidly obscene.

He should go and fetch his penknife. Instead he worked her stays loose until he could push her shift down, baring her bosom. Brown nipples, soft skin, crescent shadows beneath. He wanted to paint them for posterity. He wanted to build them a monument. Instead he cupped them with spread hands, their weight resting seductively on his fingertips. Her nipples pebbled, catching in the join of his index and middle fingers. He squeezed lightly. She strained toward him, face alight, but Sir Geoff's grip pinioned her arms. She was helpless to demand anything from Simon but what he chose to give her. Power flooded him, terribly welcome after his anxious morning.

St. Aubyn pressed against Simon's back, cupping his cock. Oh. Oh, he wanted that too. St. Aubyn's mouth was warm on his neck, and he wanted to sink into this moment until there was nothing but pleasure, until the whole world was *yes*. He wanted Sir Geoff to fuck him with his cock still wet from Maggie's cunt.

"I shouldn't stay." He dropped her breasts, relishing the cavalier cruelty of it as much as the way the globes jiggled before finding equilibrium. She liked it too; her expression bespoke nearly ecstatic frustration. "All yours, St. Aubyn." He stepped courteously past and went up the stairs without looking back.

Once in his room, he frigged himself quickly and efficiently before taking his penknife and returning down the servants' stair.

But back in the library, he couldn't recapture his concentration on his windows. Of course he couldn't.

Why did he like being cruel to her? He remembered—vividly—how he had thought of forcing himself on her in the lake yesterday. How much he had wanted to own her for a fortnight.

He'd had these thoughts before. He'd tried not to think them, and tried to forget them. Yet he could recall a few weeks at Oxford when every time he frigged himself he imagined fucking Clement while Clement struggled to get away.

It was something wrong in him, something crooked and spiteful. When he liked someone, he resented them too, for their dominion over him. He had been angry with Maggie this morning, just because he wanted to talk to her. And yet he craved that very subjection, except when he wanted to inflict it on others.

He'd hated how helpless Clement could make him feel—except in bed, where he'd loved it. Where a teasing edge in Clement's voice made him wild for more. Where he'd done whatever Clement asked.

Where he had been determined to win at last, and possess Clement for good and all. He put his face in his hands. He was a cringing, vengeful worm.

He'd told Maggie he wasn't looking for fun because he wanted to settle down. How was he supposed to settle down? Who would want to settle down with him? He was a messy child trying to pass himself off as a grown man. His parents had been parents already at his age. How would he manage with a child? When would he be able to afford one? He couldn't even afford a wife.

Meanwhile Maggie was managing a successful business *and* enjoying herself *and* being a reliable correspondent! He couldn't even remember when he'd last written to his mother. Two weeks? Three? Did she even know he was at Throckmorton?

He drew a blank piece of paper toward him. *My dearest mother...*

The letter was quite ordinary for half a page, and then he wrote, *I've met a woman. I don't*

He looked at the paper, not sure how to finish that sentence.

I don't know if I ought to tell you about her; she isn't respectable. But I respect her nevertheless, and I like her, and she's beautiful. She's Jewish and runs a faro bank. Would you still receive me if I married her?

Married her. It looked insane, in black and white.

He had never thought it was a question he would have to ask his mother. He'd assumed he would either marry a young English gentlewoman, or he'd be a confirmed bachelor with an inseparable friend (also English and of his own class) and never have to discuss the matter with his mother at all. Even if Mrs. Radcliffe-Gould heard rumors, she would never breathe a word of it to him, any more than Lady Throckmorton said a word about Clement's house parties. Simon had no idea if she knew what went on, and preferred it that way.

This couldn't be hushed up or discreetly ignored. Maggie was too well-known, too memorable. And besides, what would he do? Ask Maggie to eat pork and say she used to be a governess when they went to Yorkshire? She would tell him to go to hell.

If he did marry Maggie, would his children be strangers to their cousins? How would he explain it to them? Would it be disloyal to Maggie to go home by himself, and see his family? If he did, would it be home as it had always been, full of love and cheer, or would he be too angry to enjoy it?

Could he raise his children as Jews, and see them despised and reviled?

Why on earth would Maggie want to marry him, anyway? And on so short an acquaintance? Yet now he couldn't stop, even though every fancy brought another obstacle with it. He imagined her brightening his rooms, sharing a mug of chocolate in the morning and buttering their toast as he pulled it off the toasting fork—and then he thought that she wouldn't want to leave the club, or Meyer, and besides a gentleman with a wife was supposed to rent a house and hire a housekeeper, or at least bigger lodgings and a maid-of-all-work.

You would like her, he wrote anyway, suddenly convinced it was true. *Lively, but with her feet on the ground.* His mother was also very fond of cards, but he thought it wiser not to mention that. *Nothing is definite, and may never be*

He should burn the letter. Now, before anyone saw it.

Maggie poked her head in the door. Simon jumped. Hastily putting a period to his sentence, he signed and folded the letter without sanding it.

"How are you?" she asked. "I—I just wanted to make sure that what happened earlier was all right with you. I don't think we broke any rules, but..."

He felt a rush of gratitude—but it was not gratitude, he admitted to himself. It was infatuated adoration.

Simon laughed, his face lighting up. Maggie's stomach tightened and swooped as she remembered his hands on her breasts, and the way he had walked away from her. She had pretended afterward that St. Aubyn's hands and mouth were his, that St. Aubyn's cock was his when he pushed it into her mouth. But even with her eyes shut she had sensed every difference between them. She could distinguish their breath, even, and the shape of their hands.

Also, St. Aubyn had talked a lot.

"I don't think anyone's ever asked me that before at one of these parties," he said. "I was a bit shaken, honestly. Are *you* all right?"

She sat directly in front of his library table, propping her head and arms on the back of the sofa, and contemplated her answer. "I don't know. I enjoyed what happened, in a carnal sense. But...I don't know what to do. At first I only wanted to bed you, and I supposed I'd enjoy whatever you condescended to give me. But I...it's inconvenient and a little embarrassing, but I think I've developed a bit of a *tendre* for you." That was an understatement. How big did an understatement have to be before it was a lie? "I *want* anything you wish to give me, but perhaps it isn't prudent to *take* it. One can't always be prudent, but if things go much further, I'll start to really be hurt that you don't wish to give me more. And that wouldn't be fair to either of us."

His laugh sounded like mostly nerves this time. "How can you come right out and talk about things like that?"

Shame rushed her. "How can you rich *ingleses* never talk about *anything*?" she snapped.

"Centuries of practice?"

She couldn't stay angry. She liked him too much. "Other people talk about things more than you're used to." It came out rather flat, though she'd tried to be kind. "And I've worked at not letting shame rule me. I'm not in my teens anymore, ready to do anything to avoid a moment of mortification. Maybe I talk too much, but I only want to understand what's really going on. I find it's less embarrassing in the long run than fumbling about in the dark."

She felt a hypocrite suddenly, trying to set herself up as wiser than him. Just last week, for the millionth time, she'd thought about asking the shop-girl she always talked to at the Portuguese bakery to have tea with her, and felt too much of a fraud to do it. "And I *don't* talk about everything I should, anyway. You know that. There are a lot of things I should tell Meyer that I haven't."

He ran a hand through his hair. "You're right, fumbling around in the dark is the most uncomfortable thing in the world. But...I...How can you simply accept that you want people to be cruel to you? Isn't that something to be ashamed of? Isn't it...isn't it like turning over a rock in your mind and finding a mass of sunless crawling blind things?"

Her cheeks burned and her gorge rose. She didn't know how to push sick shame like this back except with anger, and she didn't want to be angry when he was so clearly speaking of himself, not her.

"I've wondered that myself," she said at last, her voice sounding unnatural and thick to her own ears.

He leaned forward. "I've imagined violating you," he confessed in a low voice—earnest, even apologetic.

Oh God, she was on fire.

"I wanted to treat Clement roughly sometimes, too. *Shouldn't* I be ashamed of wanting to harm someone I love?

Love ought to be kind. Not cruel."

"I don't know," she said, ignoring her stab of jealousy at the word *love*. "But here is what I do know. I want to be humiliated and ill-used. Not all the time. Only in bed. I can't stop wanting it. So what's the good in worrying about it? I—I tell everyone I'm Jewish."

He looked confused.

"And I *am*," she insisted at once. "But...I didn't know it until I was six years old and we came to England. My mother didn't know it either until a few years before that, when her own mother was on her deathbed. My grandmother's family pretended to convert so they wouldn't go to the stake. My grandmother married a Catholic, and she married my mother to a Catholic. And then my mother....she was twenty-three. She'd been a good Catholic all her life. She lost her mother and discovered she was Jewish on the same day. When her husband died too, she decided to come to England where she could really be Jewish. I'm so proud of her for that. But she never—she could never quite bring herself to do it. She doesn't go to synagogue. She never learned any prayers or songs. She follows the tradition of fasting on Mondays and Thursdays, and twice a year she has a terrible attack of conscience and spends a week crying and begging me to go to confession with her so we won't burn in a fiery pit for eternity."

She fought the urge to insist again that she *was* Jewish. He was a Gentile and he didn't care. He didn't think she was a fraud and if she said it, it would only show him that she half believed it herself. "Do you know how I met Meyer? I was in Duke's Place trying to get up the courage to go into the Great Synagogue." She hadn't even known that unmarried girls usually only went to the Great Synagogue on Purim and Simchas Torah. She'd never heard of those holidays. "He thought I was a street-walker and picked me up."

It annoyed her that he was obviously more shocked by that than by anything else she'd said. "Well, *we* think it's a charming story. Anyway, I meant that this is something that I know about myself without room for doubt: I like men to humiliate me. And anything you know about yourself, for sure, is precious." You had to cling to it, be proud of it even, because people would try to take it away from you.

He let out a long breath. "You really don't think it's different? I... I was ashamed of liking men, at first. It took me a long time to accept it. But in the end I could, because it was obvious that it did no harm. This..."

"What's the harm?"

"I'm afraid it comes from real anger, real resentment. One shouldn't resent one's friends. One shouldn't be angry at one's friends."

She couldn't smother a laugh. "Who else would one resent and be angry at, but the people one spends all one's time with?"

He blinked.

"You should try it," she said. "Not with me if you don't want to. But with somebody. It's exhilarating. When it's done right, I feel clean and new afterward. Like the light feeling after a good cry, as if all the tears and snot were in my head weighing it down." She wished she felt that way now. She wished Meyer were here.

"Catharsis," he said.

She made a face. "Isn't that...what happens when a doctor gives you a purgative? And here I hesitated to mention snot!"

"Well, yes. But in his *Poetics*, Aristotle says of tragedy..." He shut his eyes. "Pye translates it as, 'Tragedy, then, is an imitation of an important and complete action, possessing a certain degree of magnitude, in ornamented language, having its forms distinct in their respective parts, by the representation of persons acting and not by narration, effecting through the means of pity and terror the purgation of such passions.'"

The dry syllables tripped passionately off his tongue, a perfect blend of eager student and distant schoolmaster. Oh, that was charming. The tension in her spine eased.

"But Aristotle's original word was catharsis. Scholars dispute as to his precise meaning, which he doesn't explain in any extant portion of the *Poetics*. Twining renders it 'correction and refinement.' But his essential point is that sometimes playing out dreadful things serves as a kind of medicine to the mind."

"Imagine my relief that Aristotle agrees with me," she teased. "I—Simon, do you really want to treat me cruelly? Or do you want to *pretend* cruelty? To imagine cruelty? Harm me only as much as I wish to be harmed? There *is* a difference, although it took me some time to sort out, myself." She ought in fairness to have said 'people' or 'Clement', not 'me'. But she wanted him to think about doing it to her. She wanted him to long for it, as she did.

He frowned down at the library table, toying with the letter he'd been writing. When he finally looked up, her breath caught. She'd thought the cruel edge to his beauty was in the clean delicate English lines of it, like an angel in a painting. But it was more than that. When he was set on something, there was a purity of purpose to him, cold or white-hot or both at once. His gaze was like the keen edge of a knife.

"I'd endure a week of agony if it would save you a moment of unwished-for pain." He spoke in a low voice, seemingly embarrassed by his own sincerity. "I want you to know that."

Her heart gave a great, frightened bound. In a novel, that would be a proposal of marriage—though of course here, in real life, it wasn't. It was even better than *You must allow me to tell you how ardently I admire and love you*, which Maggie always thrilled to even though she would never marry a man who was so rude about *her* mother. "Th-thank you."

"I'd like to take you up to our room."

Thoughts of whether he would like Mrs. da Silva flew right out of her head. "What?"

He dipped his quill in the inkwell and began addressing his letter. *Mrs. William Radcliffe-Gould, The Rectory...*

The Rectory. She felt rather chilled. Marriage was out of the question, indeed.

"If you think it prudent," he added. "And—I hope we shall continue to further our acquaintance, when we return to London."

Her heart soared. He was telling her that this wouldn't be only one afternoon, or even only one fortnight. That was more than enough. *Much* more. She didn't want to marry him anyway. "I'd like that."

He grinned at her. "I, um, my letter has to dry and I have to light the wax jack and it's all going to take a few minutes but I really want to get this letter in the post before... I haven't written to my mother in weeks and..." He blushed. "Sorry, I'm talking too much."

"I like talking," she said. "Talking's all right." She came

round to sit on the edge of the table, sliding the elegant silver wax jack toward him. He stood, smiling down at her. She beamed back because he was going to kiss her, and it wasn't going to be a game or for show or for anything except that they both wanted to.

Neither of them could stop grinning as he leaned down and pressed his lips to hers, which should have made it difficult to kiss properly but didn't. His hands were on her shoulders. She could feel his ring through her dress.

When they stopped to catch their breaths, dust motes danced for joy in the light streaming through the windows.

"Not talking's all right too," Simon said. He reached for the desk drawer, and then kissed her again instead.

It took him half an hour to seal his letter, but at long last she watched him pass his signet twice through the jack's little flame and stamp his initials cleanly into a blob of deep red wax. Her own seal had smudged black from the flame, the wax already cracked by the time she handed the letter to Lord Throckmorton for franking.

It might have made her feel small—thinking how many more letters he'd sent than she had, and how much finer his handwriting was—but it didn't. Like watching Meyer deal cards, it was beautiful to see someone do something so well, because they had done it a thousand thousand times with love and care. It was intimate, as if by seeing this moment she was seeing all the others, as if she could see him as a little boy learning to do it for the first time.

He dropped the letter on top of hers in the salver in the entrance hall, and led her up the stairs. She caught herself trying to hide her smile, as if this were a prank they were striving to conceal. As if it mattered whether anyone knew! Glancing at Simon, she caught him doing the same thing, the corners of his mouth tucked in and a careful nonchalance in his walk. "Race you," she said, and tore up the stairs.

He was taller and probably in better condition, but less set on winning. She passed him and burst through the door of their room with her heart racing in her throat. Laughing and gasping for air, she collapsed on the bed.

Out of breath himself, he came and stood silently gazing down at her. The pounding of her heart changed as the air between them heated with possibility.

"I feel foolish trying to be masterful," he said at last. Her heart sank. Would he expect her to direct and encourage him? While she preferred that to a man who paid no mind to whether she was enjoying herself, it wasn't conducive to an illusion of helplessness. "Would you...*show* me what you like?" He hesitated. "Master me, I mean? Do you expect playacting? Harshness?"

Oh. Oh, *yes*. She stood, taking down her hair. "I enjoy a little playacting. But all that's really necessary is to tell me what to do and enjoy it, while making sure I enjoy it myself."

His blue eyes followed her hands, dilating as she unpinned her petticoats and unlaced her corset.

"Cruelty is nice if you can manage it—but please don't say anything too specific or personal. I've learned my self-love is not robust enough for nasty setdowns, even insincere ones." Pulling her shift over her head, she stood before him naked. He devoured her with his eyes, swallowing hard, but made no attempt to touch her.

The power of that coursed through her, warming her skin. "Lie down and take your cock out."

He stretched out on the bed, his elegant, confident hands smoothly unbuttoning his pantaloons despite his shallow breaths.

"Make yourself hard enough to fuck me."

He obeyed, pumping his cock with long strokes of his fist. She watched, silent, as wetness gathered between her legs. He tried to watch her too, but at last his head fell back, pleasure contorting his face.

"That's enough," she said, several strokes past enough. She climbed atop him, and without further preamble sank down onto his cock.

She closed her eyes to absorb the sensation of him inside her, the slight pain of taking him in too fast, the soft kerseymere of his pantaloons against her calves, his body quiescent beneath her while his thighs quivered eagerly.

"May I—" he began.

"No," she said sweetly. She wanted this to last, so she began with her breasts, picking them up, kneading them, toying with her nipples until she ached and glittered with pleasure. He watched her avidly, lips parted. His cock twitched inside her and his hands fisted at his sides, but he didn't touch her or move his hips. "Good boy," she said, bouncing once on his cock. His bitten-off gasp thrilled her. She put her fingers between her legs, gathering moisture before rubbing at her pearl. She let herself moan, his obvious pleasure driving hers higher. "Are you near to spending?" she asked.

"Not yet."

Thank God. She rose, rolling onto her back beside him. "Fuck me as hard as you can, but stop if you think you might spend."

He covered her at once, slamming back inside her emptiness. She reveled in the feather bed, in his coat buttons pressing into her breasts, in the powerful, controlled jerks of his hips. She spread her legs wider and shut her eyes. "Harder."

He gave her what she demanded, his own gasps and pleasure a mere unavoidable consequence of his obedience, an afterthought. She could feel his determination to please in every thrust.

All at once he stopped, his breath hot and shuddering on her neck. "I'm going to spend."

"Then pull out and use your mouth. Don't spend."

His eyes were feverish; he had to pause to collect himself, shutting his eyes and taking long breaths. He crawled backward away from her with his arse a little in the air, she guessed to keep his cock from rubbing against the sheets. Spreading her folds with his fingers, he sucked her pearl directly into his mouth. She shouted.

"Put your fingers in me," she demanded, her voice cracking. "As many as you can."

He shoved them gracelessly in and fucked her with them, his other hand coming to rest lightly on her thigh. She raised herself on her elbows to watch him, his black hair falling across his forehead and his elegant mouth working, the smooth, well-tailored line of his shoulders and the undignified hunch of his legs. The liquid heat of his tongue against her pearl had her shuddering and desperate. But still she craved something more, something darker.

She reached down to twist her hands in his hair and yank his head up. His hot eyes seared into hers, his mouth wet with her juices. "Tell me what you're going to do to me later to punish me for making you wait."

He didn't miss a beat. "Not let you put your clothes back on for dinner."

The idea was excruciating: sitting down to dinner naked. The looks, the comments. They wouldn't wait five minutes before bending her over the table and sharing her amongst themselves like a dish of potatoes. She pushed his mouth back down onto her cunt and came, screaming, a moment later.

He was breathing hard, wrung out, when she opened her eyes. She pushed him away with a foot on his shoulder. "Thanks," she said, smiling. "Now take your clothes off."

Chapter 6

Simon did as she asked. He hesitated to look at her—but when with an effort he did, her eyes were roaming over each new swath of exposed skin, so he could watch her watch him without the vulnerability of meeting her gaze.

He had never particularly admired his own naked body, and was always half surprised when lovers evinced no disappointment at it. But she said with satisfaction, "I've wanted to see this since the moment you walked into Number Eighteen," the pleasure she'd taken from him turning her voice rich and sleepy.

"Really?"

Oh, God, that was something Clement would say, and Simon had always hated it in his friend: *I wouldn't have said it if I didn't mean it.* Why hadn't he thanked her graciously? His pantaloons caught on his ankle, forcing him to hop on one foot for balance, his erection bouncing. "I mean. I only ever came to that club to see you. Well, a friend dragged me there the first time. But after that..." The pantaloons came off with a jerk and he tumbled back onto the bed.

She giggled. "Turn around and bend over the bed."

The bed was conveniently waist-height. His chest sank into the counterpane as he buried his face in his folded arms. He was relieved she couldn't see his face any longer—and dying to see what she would do to him in this vulnerable position.

He was realizing that she had been right. It was all only playacting, and what was the harm in that? He'd always loved the theater, though he was too shy to ever tread the boards himself.

Maggie's hands swept up the muscles in his back to his shoulders, and down his spine. She squeezed his arse. His cock brushed against the counterpane, an improbable bright flash of pleasure. "Please," he begged, enjoying the ragged sound of his own voice.

She spanked him lightly. "Please what?"

"Please touch my cock." His excitement grew, and with it a strange sense of liberty. He could act as pathetic and crawling as he liked just now, and she wouldn't think any the worse of him. And later—later he could act as cruel as he liked, and she wouldn't dislike him for that either. "I need it."

The playacting was half the pleasure of it, in fact. She wasn't forcing him to do anything. He wanted to be here, in this humiliating position, and she knew it. That was the most wonderfully humiliating thing of all.

He had wanted to obey her, earlier, as much as he had wanted to fuck her. He shut his eyes and remembered plunging into her welcoming flesh. He remembered her cunt clenching around his fingers as she spent.

He shivered violently when she walked her fingers down the crease of his thigh. "And if I don't?" she said.

He moved one hand down to do it himself.

Her fingers closed on his wrist, twisting his arm behind his back and forcing him to stay prone. Not hard enough to really hurt, but the blood rushed to his cock. When he turned his face to the side so he could breathe, she bent over him to say in his ear, "You don't want that." Their arms nestled between her breasts. "You want *me* to do it."

She pressed her knee between his legs, holding them apart, her thigh against his arsehole. It made his balance slip a little, made his position just a little more awkward.

Rebellion surged in him, eager to be crushed. "I don't," he said, praying she'd understand it was part of the game. "I don't want this."

She paused for a moment, weighing his sincerity; before she could ask, he thrust his hips slightly back against hers in silent invitation. She wrapped her hand around his cock at last. He pressed his forehead into the mattress and held himself taut, not sure if he was straining for orgasm or braced against it. Her hand worked him quick and unstinting, and that was better than teasing would have been. He couldn't resist it or even catch his breath and she knew. She knew he was awash with pleasure—

"It doesn't matter if you want it or not," she said conversationally, twisting his arm a little harder. "Because *I* want it, and you can't stop me. Now spend."

He gave it his best for her. Almost—

"And do it hard," she said fiercely, almost like a threat, leaning all her weight on his back. "I want to feel it."

There. His hips jerked wildly, fingers curling against her chest. She loosened her hold on his wrist but didn't let go, tethering him to the bed as pleasure racked him. Her cheek pressed against his back, to feel each tremor.

At length she kissed his shoulder and pushed herself

upright by his hips. "Was that all right?"

He was crumpled on the bed, arse in the air. Standing hastily, he scrambled for his shirt. She ogled him contentedly as he did it, though, so he didn't rush to retrieve the rest of his clothes, instead taking a seat tailor-fashion on the bed, his long shirt covering anything sensitive. "It was marvelous," he admitted.

Her eyes sparkled. "I thought so too." Less self-conscious than he, she flopped down on the bed on her stomach, feet in the air, propping her cheek on one palm to look up at him. He ran a hand over her bare back and the curve of her arse, reflecting that God was a better craftsman than humankind. The world's most exquisite temple, its most lifelike sculpture, could show no arch or contour as easy and graceful, as perfectly proportioned or pleasing to the eye. His hand slid to her thigh, fingers curling inward. It was hard to believe that a week ago, she'd been the untouchable hostess across the room at Number Eighteen, especially when she rolled onto her side to see him better, and he could see her *much* better.

But sadness crept into her face. She looked down, tracing a design on the sheet with her finger. Little hearts, he realized with a jolt. "I don't want to go home. I'm so happy here."

Hope flooded him. She wanted to stay with him, and not go back to Henney.

But it wasn't fair to be glad she was unhappy. And maybe she was only enjoying being on holiday. "I know I'm going to miss the five-course meals and the feather bed," he said carefully.

"That's part of it. But honestly..." She glanced at him and cut herself off. "I only...I *like* Number Eighteen. I love it, even.

But I've been there five nights a week for almost six years now, and...I'm bored. A *little* bored. I don't know if I can last another six years. But I don't know what else I could do! I haven't saved a penny. I couldn't even have afforded to stay in a hotel while Meyer's away. I don't know how we're to get through the summer while everyone is in the country." Her finger was tracing diamonds now. Right—cards. She was a card player. The hearts hadn't meant anything. "What if Meyer doesn't come back?" she whispered.

"What makes you think he won't?" Simon asked, surprised. He didn't hate the idea...but it occurred to him that he himself could hardly keep her in the style to which she was accustomed.

"Nothing. But you never know *what* will happen when someone visits his family abroad." She sighed. "I'm sure Mrs. Hennipzeel wants him to stay."

"Mrs. what?"

She rolled her eyes. "He goes by Henney so you Englishmen can pronounce it. But his name is Hennipzeel."

Simon giggled.

She sat up and reached for her shift. "So Hennipzeel is funny, but Skeffington isn't? Aloysius? Throckmorton?" She huffed. "*Radcliffe-Gould*," she said darkly. "Next you'll be making fun of his accent, as if you don't all talk like you have a head cold or maybe your jaws are sewn shut."

Simon felt as if she'd slapped him. She thought he sounded like his jaw was sewn shut? "So it's all very well for you to laugh at my name but I can't laugh at Henney's?" *It's not because it's foreign. It's just a funny collection of sounds. I can't help what I think is funny.* He knew none of it would appease her.

"I take it back. I can't wait to go home." Maggie laced her stays jerkily. "Five-course dinners, pfft! At least at home I can eat in peace."

He couldn't pretend not to know her meaning. Clement had let up after the visit to his mother, and even once or twice ventured a *Leave her alone,* but the other guests could not seem to stifle their curiosity—*Can you eat this? Why not?*—their helpfulness—*Oh, I don't think you can eat that, there's suet in it*—their concern—*You poor girl, aren't you hungry?*—their pity—*But oysters! How can you live without oysters?*—and, in a few cases, their thinly veiled scorn—*It's all rather Byzantine, isn't it?*

"I'm sorry," he said, defeated. "I don't know how to make them stop."

"Oh, there's no way to make them stop." It was almost dinner time now; instead of putting her day dress back on, she whisked herself into the dressing room. Simon tugged on his pantaloons and followed, watching her flip through her dinner dresses three times before shrugging and pulling out a fresh petticoat and a pink striped silk robe, which she regarded skeptically.

He wanted her to smile again, and stand near him. "Would you like to take a tray in our room tonight? I could talk to the cook."

She looked at him for the first time in minutes. "Ohhh, it's tempting." She hesitated. "No, I'm trying to make friends of the other guests so they'll come to Number Eighteen. I can't do that if I let them intimidate me."

Intimidate me. The word struck him sharply. She'd been carrying it off so well that it had never occurred to him she felt intimidated.

But perhaps that proved his own lack of imagination, not her extraordinary aplomb. To be a poor Portuguese Jew in this assembly... He searched for an analogy—and picturing himself at a hunting-and-shooting party surrounded by strapping, red-blooded, athletic types from school was unpleasant enough, even frightening, that he was abruptly swamped with guilt.

"I'm sorry," she said. "I know you didn't mean anything by it. I oughtn't to have bitten your nose off."

"No, I'm sorry. I should have apologized at once. I don't know why I didn't; I'm sorry for that too."

Her expression eased, and seeing it, so did the tightness in his chest. "Thank you. I—thank you."

"Don't thank me. Let me make it up to you."

A corner of her mouth curved. "Oh, I will. Later."

He laughed, suddenly very aware again of her breasts plumped up by her corset. How had he not been looking at them all this time? Her bare feet were adorable, and her calves. "I didn't mean *that*, though."

"If you want to make it up to me, talk up Number Eighteen to your friends."

Once again, he was impressed by her devotion to her business, when he could barely bring himself to mention his own trade to prospective customers for fear of being thought over-forward. But as business-mindedness was a quality associated with Jews, he refrained from saying so. "Having met you, I'm sure they must all be planning to go at the earliest opportunity."

"Flattery will get you nowhere." Her pleased expression belied her words.

"Perhaps we should rejoin the ladies," Simon said for the third time.

Clement blew a smoke-ring. "If you and Miss da Silva want to go upstairs, we aren't stopping you."

Guilt smote Simon. He *did* want to take Miss da Silva upstairs—an hour ago, for preference. But he was Clement's guest and he really had been ignoring him. Surely he could make it through one full evening. "Never mind. I'll have another glass of port."

Clement filled Simon's glass about twice as full as custom dictated. "Would you like a cigar?"

"Have I ever taken a cigar when you offered it to me?"

Smiling, Clement blew another smoke ring in his direction, something Simon had always found very attractive. "Yes, once, and you spent half an hour coughing."

"Perhaps we might have some singing after dinner," Simon said, missing all at once the long evenings he and Clement used to spend together at the piano.

"Let's play Magical Music," St. Aubyn suggested. "But you shouldn't spend all night at the piano yourself, Throckmorton. Let someone else have a turn so you can play." He laid a hand lightly on Clement's knee. Clement laughed flirtatiously and cut his eyes at Darling to see if he was watching.

Simon gritted his teeth. He had once been jealous of his friend's power of fascination, but with age and experience he'd realized that in addition to good looks and winsomeness, a large part of Clement's seductiveness resided in smiling at

people as if they were extraordinarily wonderful, allowing
minor liberties with his person, and listening to things that
bored him as if they didn't, all of which Simon disliked. He
found it hard to believe Clement enjoyed it either.

"Since you ask it, my dear," Clement said. "Simon, will you
play?"

This was an intentional kindness, as Simon liked playing
the piano and disliked Magical Music. The game required one
member of a party to leave the room, while the rest determined
a task for him to perform when he returned—for example,
removing flowers from a vase. The person at the piano then
provided hints by playing louder when the player neared the
vase, softer when he lost the scent, and so on. As with most
parlor games, it revolved around being watched and laughed
at, and played in this company, all the tasks would be scandalous if not actually obscene.

Simon gulped down his port. "If Miss da Silva is not too
tired, certainly."

When the gentlemen at last rejoined the ladies, Maggie's
eyes met Simon's at once. He wanted nothing more than to
take her upstairs.

"We mean to play Magical Music," Clement announced.
"Do you agree, ladies?"

Simon crossed to Maggie's side. "They're bound to require
you to come into intimate contact with one or another of the
guests. Would you rather retire?"

She looked around the room. Everyone was already whis-
pering suggestively to one another. "I would probably enjoy it.
But I don't mind retiring. I imagine this was the sort of thing
you brought me so as to avoid."

It was, and yet he had found a reluctant pleasure in evenings like this, once. Perhaps if he tried again—without using Clement's insistence as an excuse he was grateful for, yet resented—he would find the pleasure greater. He had liked watching her with Sir Geoff and St. Aubyn. "Let's stay."

He took his place at the piano, and the game proceeded apace: St. Aubyn kissed Sir Geoff, Sir Geoff fondled Miss Abrami's bosom, etc., each command growing in daring until Darling said, "Miss da Silva hasn't been in play yet. I say Miss O'Leary kisses her cunny."

Her eyes flew to Simon's, hot with desire. "If Radcliffe-Gould doesn't mind," she said demurely. Her tone told him it was part of the game. She wanted him to be the one to yield her up. The atmosphere in the room already had him half-hard, despite his lingering embarrassment—or maybe partly because of it. At this, he stiffened further.

You'll be wet and ready for me when I take you upstairs. He imagined saying it aloud. "No objection," he said blandly.

Miss O'Leary was let back into the room. The young woman stood before each member of the party in turn, Simon's soft reel falling off when she stopped. Then she came to Maggie, and Simon plunked out a few swift chords.

Miss O'Leary swept her hands through the air, shaping at a distance Maggie's head, shoulders, breasts, and hips. When she neared her feet, Simon eased his foot half off the soft pedal, watching Maggie's breathing quicken in anticipation. Finally Miss O'Leary understood she was to lay her hands on the hem of her skirts. She drew them up Maggie's stockinged legs and over her bare thighs as Simon played louder. St. Aubyn whispered something in Clement's ear, and Clement laughed. Sir

Geoff looked jealous. Were he and St. Aubyn—? But Simon would have to attend to gossip another time.

Maggie kept her legs primly together and took her skirts, holding them out of the way. Simon released the soft pedal as Miss O'Leary drew her legs apart. People giggled and called out encouragement. From this angle Miss O'Leary blocked everything from Simon's sight except Maggie's stockinged knees and a sliver of bare thigh to either side.

He switched back to *due corde* as Miss O'Leary's hands slid up her thighs. "So not my hands, then." Miss O'Leary mimed sticking her elbow up Maggie's cunt.

Simon laughed with everyone else as she pulled Maggie to the edge of the chair.

Maggie watched Miss O'Leary's head dip between her thighs, sucking in a breath as her mouth touched her.

Simon pressed the damper pedal, allowing the last notes to linger a few extra seconds for her sake as he took his hands from the keyboard. Maggie let her skirts fall, flushed and laughing.

"All right, Miss da Silva, out of the room," Darling ordered good-naturedly. "It's your turn."

"I think it just *was* my turn," she said. "I'd like Mr. Radcliffe-Gould to set my task, if you don't mind." And she disappeared out the door.

Heat swept over Simon.

"Well?" Clement said.

He couldn't think of anything he had any particular desire to see. But he supposed that wasn't the point. She wanted to know *he* had commanded her to do whatever it was she was doing.

"Perhaps she might sit in Palliser's lap for half a minute," he suggested.

"I've certainly no objection," Palliser said.

Maggie found her target easily. But she could not sort out what she was supposed to do with him. Simon played quieter and quieter, watching Palliser's smug excitement grow. After standing puzzled a moment, she threw up her hands and straddled him, looking to Simon in exasperation.

"Allow me to take pity on you, madam." Palliser turned her hips with his hands, settling her in his lap. "You must keep the position half a minute, now." Pulling her arse snug against his cock, he reached into his own breeches to place his cock where he wanted it. Her lips parted, startled, and her eyes fixed on Simon's.

Every stroke of Simon's fingers on the keys gave his consent to Maggie's degradation as Palliser rubbed himself against her arse, his hands wandering. Simon silently counted to thirty—and then dragged it out a few more seconds, because he was enjoying himself.

She stood, biting her lip. "Perhaps we ought to begin making the tasks longer before we all expire of frustration." Behind her, Palliser's arousal was visible to everyone in the room.

Simon had had his fill of frustration. He stood. "Actually, I will be taking Miss da Silva out on the balcony before *I* expire of frustration."

"No need to go so far," Clement said. "You may take her on the sofa if you like."

God help him, he wanted to. He wanted everyone to crowd around, touching themselves, perhaps touching him.

You don't know most of these people, he reminded himself.

You don't trust them. Clement might think it means something. Tomorrow you'll wish you hadn't. He had gone far enough tonight. He wanted to learn to chart a middle course between all and nothing.

"The balcony will suit us admirably." He dragged her outside, pulling the curtains and French doors shut behind them. "Get on your hands and knees. And keep quiet. I don't want them to hear us."

He knelt between her legs on the hard stone, throwing up her skirts to display, dimly, the pale globes of her arse. A hand between her legs revealed her wetness. She cried out at once, squirming.

He toyed with her until he could bear it no longer, and then he pushed his pantaloons down and drove into her. Oh, *God.* She was wet and tight and unbelievably hot. He put his hand to the back of her neck, holding her roughly down while he fucked her. She writhed helplessly against him. "Take it," he said between his teeth, plowing into her until his ballocks slapped against her tender flesh.

"Yes," she sobbed softly. "Anything. Anything, just don't stop."

He bent lower, reaching between her thighs. He could not get over how much he loved this. Her pleasure was his; she could not deny it him. When he pinched her clitoris between his fingertips, her thighs trembled. Wonder and hot triumph mingled in his chest as he felt her pleasure.

"I wonder how many men would have to fuck you, one after the other, before you begged them to stop." He barely knew what he was saying anymore, but she'd loved the idea of going down naked to dinner. "Could you take everyone here? We'll tie your legs open in the drawing room as a public convenience."

She cried out and spent. He fucked her through it, feverish with exultation, then sank down on the ground. *Ow*. His knees ached. "Come here." She turned, crawling toward him on unsteady legs. He took her by the hair and pushed her down on his cock.

She moaned weakly when he hit the back of her throat. God, she liked that too.

Time blurred. How long had he been fucking her mouth? Just as he began dimly to fear he would really tire her too far, she took his cock in one hand and his ballocks in the other, working him swiftly to his peak.

He half-sat, half-lay on the stone balcony, the night air cold against his sweaty skin. "Good Christ," he said dazedly.

"Let's go to bed," she said. "And let's take some wine with us."

Faintly, somewhere in the house, a clock chimed three. Maggie had been asleep for an hour. Simon couldn't sleep. He couldn't stop thinking of his letter to his mother, waiting in the entrance hall below.

Marry her? Was he crazy? He'd known her a week. He'd known her a week and he loved her already and when the letter came back from his mother saying she would never be received at the Rectory, Maggie would show him the door.

He shouldn't rush this, anyway. She'd agreed to see him when they went back to London. That was enough for now.

He'd only frighten her off if he was too eager.

And what if he told his mother, and then Maggie turned him down? He'd have to tell Mrs. Radcliffe-Gould, and she would be relieved, and he would be so angry.

How could he trust himself to marry anyone, anyway? Five years ago, he'd have married Clement if he could have, and now he'd be miserable. What had he been thinking of, writing that letter? He had to get it back before the footman posted it in the morning.

At last Simon rose, put on his dressing gown and slippers, and crept downstairs. He dug through the letters in the dark. Which one was his? In the end he gathered them all up and felt his way to the library door.

But when he opened it, the dark library wasn't empty. A lamp illuminated a small circle around one of the tables. Clement sat in its glow, reading letters with his glasses perched on his nose. He was too vain to wear them where anyone could see. Simon had been the one exception to that rule, once; it had felt like such a gift.

"Simon?" Clement peered at him. "Did you want a book?"

He stepped forward into the light. "I wanted to add an enclosure to my letter to my mother," he said, knowing how stupid it sounded. "What are you doing?"

Clement laughed, a little sheepishly, taking his glasses off. "Oh, you know. I suppose I should be in the study, but it still feels like Father's. One of the tenants has got himself up before the justice of the peace for sheep-stealing, and I'm trying to save his neck."

Clement was up late handling estate business? But then, it made sense. He probably wouldn't want any of his guests to know, any more than he'd want them to see his glasses. "Do you think he's innocent?"

"Oh, I'm quite sure he isn't. I'm going to have to charm the JP somehow and ask him to sort it out as a personal favor. I'll invite him over to shoot next week. I suppose I'll have to talk to the man who owned the sheep, too..."

"You hate shooting."

Clement smiled mischievously. "Hopefully my incompetence will give him a comfortable sense of superiority, and then he'll be as clay in the hands of the potter. I'm reading his correspondence with Father to prepare myself."

And just like that, Simon loved him again. Longed for him, wanted to throw himself into his arms.

He wanted this to be over, to be behind him—and yet the idea terrified him. If he could stop loving Clement, then maybe one day he'd look at Maggie and feel nothing too. He fumbled through the morning's post, looking for his.

"What's really in the letter?" Clement asked.

Simon hesitated. "Can I talk to you about Maggie? I want to, but not if it will hurt you."

"Please," Clement said at once. "I'm dying to know what's going on."

"I told my mother about her in the letter. I said—I said I was thinking about asking her to marry me."

Clement looked blank.

"But it's too soon," Simon hurried on. Should he have lied? Clement had *said* he wanted to know. "It's mad. I can't send a letter like that. Mother's bound to write back that she and my sisters wouldn't receive her. I'd have to tell her, because it would be dreadful not to, but what kind of thing is that to drop on someone after only a few weeks? 'Stick with me, and you'll get insults instead of a family'?"

Clement's eyebrows rose to the ceiling. "And here I thought you left me because *I* was too scandalous."

"You thought—?" He felt awful. Clement thought he'd broken it off because he was ashamed of him? Because he wanted to be respectable? "But I *told* you why I left."

"Yes, but it didn't make any sense." Clement began to tap his glasses agitatedly against his stack of correspondence. "You said we wouldn't make each other happy, but we *were* happy. You were happy. Much happier than you are now."

Simon blinked. Had he been? No. No, of course not. The truth hit him: Clement only saw him when he was around Clement, and he hadn't been happy much around Clement in a long time. He was afraid to be, these days, for fear Clement would think it was an invitation. "I wasn't. I'm sorry, but—"

"Never mind," Clement interrupted. "Never mind, I don't want to hear about her after all. It's too painful. It's too painful just to be here with you and know I can't ever have you again. Maybe—maybe we just shouldn't see each other anymore. We could still correspond, but..."

Simon could not quite breathe. "Not see each other anymore? Ever?"

Clement straightened the stack of papers in front of him with trembling hands. "I don't know. Maybe not."

He couldn't seem to collect his thoughts. Never seeing Clement again? The last twelve years of his life, gone without a trace? "How can you say that to me? I thought—I thought we were friends! And just because I won't fuck you anymore you don't want to *see* me?"

Was it his imagination, or did Clement look pleased to have got a reaction? "We're both very tired. Let's talk about it in the morning, when we're calmer."

Simon, stiff with fear and fury, didn't trust himself to answer. He might say something that really couldn't be patched up. Instead he stormed out, promptly stubbing his toe on the stairs and spending several moments cursing violently under his breath.

Once back in his room, he stood in the dark for long minutes, afraid that if he got into bed his pounding heart would wake Maggie.

He became aware that the letter was still clutched in his hand. He shoved it to the bottom of his trunk to deal with in the morning.

"Simon?" Maggie said sleepily. "What are you doing?"

"I—I forgot something downstairs. And then I had a quarrel with Clement."

He could hear her roll over. "Why was Clement even downstairs at this hour? Is the party still going on?"

He crawled into bed. "No, he was working." He couldn't bring himself to tell her what Clement had said. It would make it real, and anyway she didn't like Clement and wouldn't understand why it was so terrible.

"I'm sorry. Come here." She slung her arm over his waist and curled up against him, her nose poking his spine. He put his hand over hers, and to his complete surprise, felt much less like a smashed egg.

Simon rose early the next morning. He burned the letter in the breakfast-room fire, afraid all the time that Maggie would walk in, before sitting down to toast and chocolate. Clement poked his head in soon after, took two cups, and filled them both with coffee.

They didn't discuss what had happened. In fact, Clement talked about the radical demonstrations in the north as if nothing had happened. Simon told himself they had just both been angry, and went along with it.

Another week passed like a dream for Maggie. She felt continually drunk with delight. Simon took her to bed three or four times a day, and in between, they continued to find hours of things to say to one another. One afternoon she read a novel start to finish while he sketched with a straight ruler and compass; she couldn't remember the last time she'd been so happy.

She was on her way to breakfast one morning, hoping to catch Simon still there, when a footman brought the letter. It was from Meyer, who had sealed it with a truly enormous lump of wax to keep it safe for its long journey. Maggie repaired to the library for a letter-opener.

It was the longest letter she'd ever got from him, taking up the entire page with the last few lines crammed into minuscule print and the signature curling up the right margin. But there didn't seem to be anything in it of note. She skimmed a description of his Aunt Roosje's gefilte fish, an account of a quarrel between his uncles over his late father's best suit, and sighed in relief when she saw, *I sail for home Thursday sennight.* Then she read the next sentence.

I don't know quite how to tell you this, Magdele, but I'm bringing a wife with me.

Maggie felt as if she'd swallowed a rock. The page blurred before her eyes, and it was several seconds before she could keep reading.

I don't think it will change things much. Gittel's a broad-minded young woman who wants to come to England and not have to cover her elbows and fuss about Saturday. I've been honest. She's excited to meet you and wants to play the piano at Number Eighteen and bake for our guests. Her money should buy the pianoforte and get us through the summer.

And then he'd run out of space and signed his name. She couldn't help thinking that he'd filled up the whole page with inconsequentialities on purpose, to have an excuse to stop writing. Coward.

But why was she so angry? If she had been bored at Number Eighteen, and eager to make another connection, why shouldn't he do the same? What did it matter that Mrs. Hennipzeel approved of this Dutch girl whose morals sounded no stricter than Maggie's own, while she still didn't know Maggie existed?

Would she and Meyer still be best friends? Or would his wife come by insensible degrees to hold that place? And Maggie couldn't share a room with a married couple. She'd have to sleep in the club-room, and knock before she went into her own room for breakfast or a shawl.

Could she live with Simon? But their connection was still so young. She wanted to let it open like a rose, at its own pace, not cram herself into his lodgings out of necessity.

She wanted to talk to Simon, and have him reassure her, but it would be rude to tell him how sad she felt, when he was already jealous of Meyer. She went looking for him anyway.

Simon was just pouring himself some chocolate when Clement came into the breakfast room. It struck him suddenly that Clement always seemed to walk in just as he was sitting down to breakfast. He tried to believe it was a coincidence, and that Clement hadn't asked a footman to alert him when Simon appeared downstairs.

At least today he didn't look as if he'd just dragged himself out of bed. He smiled when Simon wished him good morning, but a worried frown lingered on his brow. "Do you know anything about cows?"

"Not a thing."

Clement sighed. "Neither do I. My steward just talked to me about them for half an hour, and..." He gave an appealing look. "Simon, do you promise not to be angry if I tell you something?"

He'd never liked Clement's habit of saying that. Until today, though, he'd always promised, since he never let himself be angry with Clement anyway. "You know I can't anticipate what my feelings will be. I'll try not to shout."

"I can't afford the folly," Clement said in a rush.

Simon set down his toast, his stomach starting to roil. "Pardon?"

"I can't afford the folly. I shouldn't have commissioned it in the first place, but I thought I could find the money and I wanted to see you. It's so strange being here without Father, and you never visit me unless I bribe you."

Simon felt guilty, and resented it. He rose from his chair,

demanding, "So now it's *my* fault you wasted my time?"

Clement's cheeks flushed. "I wasted your *time*? That's rich. You've enjoyed yourself, haven't you, at my expense? Where else would you have taken Miss da Silva? To your closet in London? To visit your *parents*, maybe?"

"I only brought her in the first place to keep *you* at arm's length!" Simon paused, shocked at himself, but too angry to stop. "Because you can't seem to understand that you aren't entitled to my company will-I-nill-I. If I don't wish to visit you, then you ought to do without me, instead of *lying* to get me here when I could have been working on a paying commission. I've got less than twenty pounds in the bank, for God's sake! I need the money."

Clement drew back in shock. "I didn't realize. Of course you can stay here until you've found another patron—"

"Are you *joking*?"

"Mona, I didn't lie. I thought I could find the money. I missed you."

"I didn't miss you." Simon should leave the dining room and slam the door behind him. There was nothing left to say. But he wanted there to be. He wanted to achieve catharsis: to feel purged and purified, a weight lifted. But he was only here, hot and trembling and as angry and unhappy as he'd been before.

Clement turned abruptly and hurried out of the door he'd come through. Simon did feel light, now. Too light, sickeningly so, as if the person he'd been for the last dozen years had vanished, and left very little behind.

They'd have to leave Throckmorton at once. What would Maggie think of his rooms in London? How would he be able to sleep without her in the bed next to him? He sensed that empty-eggshell loneliness waiting to hollow him out.

How was he to get another commission now everyone had left town for the summer?

He needed to have a drink, talk to Maggie, and pack his trunk, in that order. He couldn't think about what would come after that.

Chapter 7

Maggie could hear Simon and Lord Throckmorton quarreling in the breakfast room next door. Should she stop it? In the end she felt too tired and afraid. She curled up on the sofa and tried to compose a congratulatory letter to Meyer.

The sound of the door opening frightened her for no good reason. She bolted upright as Simon came in, looking white and miserable.

"Simon, what is it?"

He went straight to the brandy decanter and poured himself a generous glass. Knocking half of it back didn't noticeably steady him. The black hair falling over his forehead looked lank and stringy with unhappiness.

She stood, her heart going out to him. "What did he say?"

"He isn't going to build a ruin after all," he said in a low voice. "I don't know how I'm to support us until my next commission. Why did I come here in the first place? Only because I was too lazy and cowardly to try to drum up business elsewhere." He swallowed the rest of his brandy. "I have no judgment or instincts. Why do I listen to Clement over and over and over again?"

Maggie felt very small. She'd seen young men about town run out of money before. "Are you going home to your parents?" Yorkshire was so far away, and probably he'd forget her by the time he came back. Maybe he'd come back with a wife.

"I can't. They can't know I'm out of money. My father thinks I picked this profession because I'm an idler, and he's not wrong. I've made a hash of my life."

Maggie was feeling panicked and thin-skinned, and she would have liked someone to take care of *her* just now, instead of being obliged to make him feel better. But that was unfair, and not his fault. "You're not lazy or cowardly," she said, as patiently as she could. "You just—"

"No, I am." He sat on the edge of a sofa, one at rather a distance from hers, and dragged a shaking hand through his hair. His eyes burned into her with a sincerity so bright and hot it gave her vertigo, like looking at the shimmering pavement in summer. "You should know what you're getting into. I can't—I tried to tell my mother about you, and I couldn't. I crept downstairs and took the letter out of the post in the middle of the night, because I knew—I wanted to marry you."

She could feel the blood drain from her face. "What?" she said weakly.

"I had thought of one day asking you to marry me," he qualified, but even that was so startling as to render her speechless. "But I have nothing to offer you. No family. No steady income. My lodgings are half the size of yours."

She stood, wanting to *do* something, but there wasn't anything to do. She paced to the French doors and looked out at the beautiful grounds. "Simon, I don't care about the money. But we've only really gotten to know each other in the last week and a half. I can't—I don't—"

"Had the idea not even occurred to you?" he asked in a small voice.

"I—yes, but only as an idle daydream." Now that he was really saying it, she was terrified. She didn't want this to end, but she couldn't marry him. Give up Meyer and everything she knew and spend all her time in places like this that shut her out? "Our children—you wouldn't want to raise your children as Jews."

"I don't know," he said, and that surprised her speechless too. He might? "I've thought of all the obstacles. My parents wouldn't receive us, I don't think, unless you were baptized, and your reputation—well, they couldn't, for my sisters' sake, and my father's parishioners would probably—I always wanted my children to have a big, happy family, and—"

Maggie couldn't breathe for how much it hurt. "Baptized? I *was* baptized, you, you—I'd *never* do it again, not for anyone!"

"I know," he said at once, but she didn't feel better. Every word he'd said felt branded into her chest. She had always wanted her children to have a big, happy family, too. A *Jewish* one. Maybe it wasn't possible. She had no one but her mother, so her husband would have to supply the deficit. Meyer was getting married to someone else, who didn't have Maggie's reputation, and what family-minded Jewish man would want her?

What family-minded Jewish men was she likely to meet, anyway, living as she did? Instead here she was, wanting this *inglês* so badly that losing him felt like water flooding her nose and mouth.

"So you really never thought this might be forever?" he asked.

She shook her head.

"Then why are we wasting our time?"

"I don't know."

He stood, looking worse than when he came in. "I'm going to order our carriage back to London. I'm sorry I dragged you here for nothing."

Nothing. She wouldn't, until a moment ago, have called this week nothing. But maybe it was.

Simon ordered the carriage, and asked the butler to have the cook make up a hamper, and generally put off going upstairs to pack his things as long as he could. He couldn't face Maggie looking at him. He had nothing left, and she knew it; he loved her, and she'd really never wanted more than to enjoy herself for a few weeks, just as she'd told him in the beginning.

But when he finally did go upstairs, he found her sitting on her trunk sobbing brokenly. Shock speared through him. "Maggie? What's the matter?"

She turned red eyes on him. "I don't want it to be over." Her face was crumpled and wet and there was a big damp patch on her white sleeve. "I adore you and Meyer's getting married to some Dutch girl and I—I've always had this stupid daydream that I'll marry a nice Jewish man, and I'll go to synagogue with him, and we'll celebrate all the holidays at home and his family will take me in and love me and love our children and then, finally, I'll really be Jewish. It's laughable. The truth is no one is *ever* going to want to introduce me to his mother. I'm the one that's made a hash of my life."

Her tears started afresh, torrents of them. "I just—I never think. I never even thought that this was a waste of time if we weren't going to be forever, because I never think of the future at all. I've worked so hard for years, I've earned so much money, and what do I have to show for it? Not a penny. *Nothing.* An enormous wardrobe no one would even want to buy from me!"

She had seemed so calm in the library. He had never dreamed she was so upset. It shoved him out of his own panic, somehow. He had been thinking only of himself, of his own hurt, of his own failure. He'd behaved as if he couldn't hurt her, but he had. Henney's mother didn't know who she was, Simon remembered suddenly, and he'd gone on about his family rejecting her as if it would only make her despise *him*, and not as if she would be hurt, or humiliated.

In the face of her tears, and how much he wanted to put his arms around her, and *I adore you*, the problems that had loomed so large a moment ago seemed awfully unimportant. He thought about never introducing her to his sisters, and he thought about never seeing her again, and the second idea was so much worse it was almost amusing.

He knelt on the floor by her trunk, taking her hands in his. He could taste her tears when he kissed them. "You know, we're neither of us very practical people. But I think—I think practicality is what we need right now."

She pulled her hands away. "What are you talking about?"

He slid down to sit cross-legged at her feet. "This last fortnight, you've made me see that I can be very all or nothing. I thought it had to be marriage, right now, or this is a waste of time. But it doesn't feel like a waste of time, does it?"

She shook her head, sniffling.

"I think we ought to take it one step at a time. Everything we've talked about is a practical obstacle. We haven't much money, and my family probably wouldn't receive us, and you want Jewish children, and my friends will talk about how you eat, and all that. If you think..."

He was so afraid to say this, so afraid she would say there was no point to trying, because she would never want to spend her life with him. "Think about whether you might want to settle down with me. You don't have to say you *will*. You're right, it's far too soon for that. But if you could see it as a possibility, I believe we can solve all the other things, step by step." He took a deep breath. "If you don't, then let's say goodbye when we get to London." He could hardly believe he'd said it; for so long he had taken love on any terms. But he couldn't do that anymore.

Her green eyes glittered, hopefully, through her wet lashes. Her embroidered petticoat fluttered at him. He wanted to put his head on her knee and be surrounded by it. What if this was his last chance? "And I don't mind if all you've got is your wardrobe," he added. "It's a splendid wardrobe."

She laughed, and blew her nose in a flowered handkerchief. He loved her so much. "I—I don't know. I have to think about it."

He stood up. "I'm going to go do something practical about my bank balance. Think about it while I'm gone." He didn't want to leave the room without an answer. But he made himself do it anyway.

Maggie thought about it. Simon, forever. It sounded wonderful if she ignored every other consideration—which was precisely what she'd been doing.

She had thought herself so daring, so smart, but now that she was faced with maybe losing Meyer, she had to admit that she hadn't been, not really. She'd relied on him to make overtures to her lovers, to make her Jewish—to choose her clothes, even! She loved the clothes, but that wasn't the point. She'd built a whole wardrobe, a whole *life*, that only made sense in the context of somebody else, and she'd let it trap her. She'd gotten so good at saying yes and no that she hadn't noticed those were only answers to other people's questions.

She kept thinking, *If Meyer were here I wouldn't feel so afraid.* She wanted to find a way to be feel all right on her own.

Until now, she hadn't even quite realized she secretly believed that only getting married would at last make her Jewish for good and all. That she couldn't do it alone.

It's only a practical obstacle, she told herself. *I can solve it step by step.*

She took out her pencil and sat at the writing table. *Ways to be Jewish on my own,* she wrote.

1. Make Jewish friends. Women friends, too. Under that she wrote, *Finally ask that girl at the Portuguese bakery if she'd like to go for a drink sometime.*

2. Go to synagogue every Purim and Simchas Torah, even if Meyer isn't in the mood. Talk to the other women instead of just trying to pretend you know all the words.

3. Maybe Meyer's wife will teach me some things.

She couldn't think of anything else at the moment. But that was a start.

Everything on the list frightened her. All this time she'd told herself she was brave, but she'd never really gambled much, had she? Not when she didn't have Meyer stacking the deck.

Some of those women would turn up their noses at her, but she could bear that. Some of them wouldn't.

Some of them must be like her.

The thought startled her, but it had to be true. Somewhere in London—probably right where she'd grown up, actually—there were other women who'd been robbed of their faith, and were trying to get it back. She could find them if she looked.

So there was the first practical obstacle sorted.

Did she think she could manage forever with Simon Radcliffe-Gould? She didn't know. But she knew that giving up and accepting forever without him would be a damned shame.

Clement wasn't hard to find. He had locked himself in the music room and was playing *The Magic Flute* very loudly on the piano. About two-thirds of his guests were standing outside pleading with him, to no apparent effect.

Simon had to shout to be heard over the noise. "Clement? It's Simon. Let me in."

Clement played louder.

At least Simon could hear him. "You go away," he told everyone. "I'll deal with it." He was not particularly impressed when Darling left with the others, but then, nothing Darling had done had impressed him yet. "Clement, it's just me now. I'm going to sit down and wait for you to open the door, all right?" He leaned his back against the door and waited.

Clement banged through the song and one more for good measure. Silence reigned for long minutes. Simon was about to threaten to break the door down when Clement opened it, his eyes red and swollen. "You might as well come in."

"I'm sorry." Simon squeezed in beside Clement on the piano bench. "I was an ass."

"You meant every word."

"I did," he admitted. "But I could have been kinder about it."

"I can't help it that I still love you."

"Maybe not. But you could help trying to trick me into coming to your party."

"I meant to pay for the ruin!"

"I know, but I thought you actually *wanted* a ruin. You don't have to pay me to spend time with you. You just have to accept that it won't be every day anymore."

Clement picked out a sad tune on the piano.

Simon screwed his courage to the sticking point. He'd never dared ask this before, in case he got an answer he didn't like. "Clement, *do* you want to be friends?" He'd thought Clement's no-visiting threat was intended as a punishment, to hurt him. Maybe it had been. But he admitted now that if Clement had been unfair, so had he. "You don't owe me friendship any more than I owe you love. If it really is too painful—I'll understand. I'll be sorry, but I'll understand."

"Yes. Yes, I want to be friends. I was just angry."

Simon let out a breath. "I'm not going to always give way anymore," he warned. "When we disagree, sometimes I'm going to stick to my guns."

"You make me sound so unreasonable," Clement said. "Of course I don't always expect to have my own way."

Simon let it pass. For the first time he acknowledged to himself that it would never be like it had been between them. Now there was distance, where once they had been too close to catch their breaths. That was all right. It was *good*.

Maybe it was too late to patch things up at all. He hoped not—but for the first time, the idea of losing Clement didn't provoke blind, desperate terror.

He'd been afraid of never feeling about anyone again the way he had about Clement. But now he loved Maggie, and it was a promise and a benediction. He hoped to love her forever, hated the idea he might not—but he could concede (reluctantly) that if one day they separated, he would probably love someone else afterward. There was no one chance at happiness, no single destined person one either found or spent one's life missing.

Even if he was lonely for a while, he could get through it, one step at a time.

"Did you really bring Miss da Silva to fend me off?" Clement asked. He was already preening a little, between sniffles, at this idea of his own importance.

"Yes," Simon admitted.

"But you're fucking her."

"I wasn't when we arrived. I thought if I did, it would be a distraction from my work."

Clement snorted.

"You know how easily distracted I am!"

"You'd have graduated with a First if it wasn't for me," Clement said, "but you'd have had a lot less fun."

"I don't know. I've told myself the same thing, but I was never as hard a worker as I thought. I just let you take the blame for slacking my studies." Simon tried to imagine university without Clement. He didn't care about the First, but would he have been happier? Would he have found friends who demanded less? Or would he merely have spent three years huddled alone in his room?

He remembered his secret shame, thinking Clement had picked him because he didn't have other friends. But the truth was, he'd chosen Clement the same way. He *had* had other friends, but Clement was always available. If Simon happened to want someone to talk to, or dine with, or to go to the theater with, Clement had never said no. They had spent every day in the week together—because they had liked each other, certainly, but also because they had both been uncertain boys who hated solitude.

"Clementine, you really ought to get rid of Darling. If you've got to have somebody, St. Aubyn would take his place like a shot, and he's much nicer."

Clement's playing turned sulky. "Sir Geoff is in love with St. Aubyn."

"That isn't your problem."

Clement smiled. "You're so ruthless on my behalf. But it is my problem, I'm afraid. I—I like Sir Geoffrey, actually."

Ah. The quiet, less confident one. Simon supposed he shouldn't be surprised. He put a hand to the keys, picking out a slow harmony. "Are you sure he cares for St. Aubyn as more than a friend? All I've noticed is that he doesn't like St. Aubyn talking to *you*."

Clement's fingers trilled hopefully up into the high octaves.

"Do you think so?"

"It can't hurt to make an overture."

"It can always hurt to make an overture," Clement said drily.

Simon laughed. They were playing together now, and it made him feel surprisingly strong, as if the music were being drawn into his hands instead of coming out of them. "You should try it anyway."

Clement shrugged. "Maybe I will." He played softer, almost shyly. "If you marry Miss da Silva..." he said, and trailed off. Simon waited, nervous, but Clement said, "She'll have a brother," and looked very hard at the keys.

Simon was seized with affection. "Thank you," he said sincerely, bumping Clement's shoulder with his own even though he didn't know that Maggie would be too thrilled to hear it.

Would he think of Henney as a brother, someday? It was hard to imagine—hard, even, not to feel a certain distaste at the idea, though he was ashamed of it. But probably brothers-in-law were always a tricky prospect. "I need your help," he said.

Maggie had finished packing her trunk and was sitting on it impatiently, trying to decide whether she felt justified in purloining a half-read novel from Throckmorton's library, when Simon returned. Looking at him with one beautiful hand on the door and an uncertain twist to his narrow mouth, she knew she'd made the right decision. She wanted to blurt it out—no, she wanted to wait for him to speak first. She made herself blurt it out anyway.

"If you don't expect me to convert, and you don't mind our children being Jewish—" She hesitated. "That is, I know you may want to celebrate your holidays with them. But it can't be only that. I can't—I want them to have what I didn't. To grow up knowing our prayers and having friends like themselves." *Meyer's children,* she thought, with a bittersweet, hopeful pang. Her kids would have that big family, she promised herself. One way or another. "If you're willing to sort all that out, then I want to see if forever is a possibility. With you. I—"

Gladness transformed his face. Words didn't seem like enough, suddenly. She went to him and kissed him, almost crying again with how relieved she felt, how happy, to feel his mouth against hers. She could feel herself lighting up inside like a chandelier, one small candle after another.

"I spoke to Clement," he said, his smile breaking out, "and he talked to St. Aubyn with me. I showed him my design for the ruin. He loved it, and he's going to buy it for his place in Kent. I don't know why I didn't just do that at once, instead of throwing up my hands and bemoaning my fate. I'm sorry I hurt you."

"I'm sorry I hurt you too. I'm sorry I didn't take you seriously, only because you were English."

He hooked a finger in her sash. His eyes gleamed happily, slicing right into her, and it felt wonderful. "I told you I'd endure a week of agony if it would save you a moment of unwished-for pain," he said. "But do you remember when you said, *Who else should one be angry at but one's friends*? I think...I think that if we wish to be closer to each other than anyone, we shall likely cause each other more pain than anyone. Just as a consequence of proximity. It's hard to reconcile myself to the idea. I'm sorry I laughed at Henney's name. I'm sorry I let my pride rule me, and make me think I must offer you money, or a house, or a family, or anything more than just myself. I'm so sorry I said that, about your reputation, and my fathers' parishioners. I'm sorry I didn't credit you with an ordinary human capacity for hurt and fear, only because you're brave. I wish I could promise not to hurt you again, but I suppose I will. I can only promise you that I'll always be sorry. I'll always try to make it up to you. And I'll always love you."

Maggie blazed with light. "Offer me yourself. I'll take it."

"St. Aubyn's given me an advance and offered to let us go at once to his property to draw up proper plans. Will you go to Kent with me?"

"Yes," she said, and then wanted to say more. Wanted to be the one asking, finally.

I do, actually, want to find someone who'll ask me to marry them, he'd said a lifetime ago, and she'd thought it was so sweet. "And—of course it's too soon to talk about forever. But let's, this year, look at the problems one after another, and find solutions. And in a year, if I still feel about you how I do now, I'll ask you to marry me."

He crushed her to him and held her tight. "I'd like that," he said into her hair.

There was one more thing she was afraid to say. She made herself say it, her cheek pressed against his coat. "I've never even been faithful to a man before. I don't know if I'll like it."

He let her go, and there was a silence. She held her breath. "Do you think, between us, faithfulness might mean something other than strict chastity?" he asked hesitantly. "I don't see why holding our own connection sacred should prevent us from, possibly, forming others. I don't—" He laughed, ducking his head. "The truth is, Maggie, that I hope you won't expect me to go at the pace I've been going forever. You may want other company to satisfy you, after a while."

Relief flooded her. If he did not mean, by marriage, what people commonly expected it to mean—if he was willing to negotiate—if he did not begrudge her freedom—maybe they *could* have forever.

He bit his lip. "I think part of why I set my heart on marriage so soon, was because I'm afraid you *won't* feel the same in a year. That your feelings will change, and then there'll be nothing holding you to me. It's small of me."

I'm behaving like Clement, he meant. She knew him so well already. In a year, she would know him much better. For a second she thought, *Get the ring on your finger before he comes to his senses.* What a pair they were!

"I don't think they'll change," she said impulsively. "I think—I think they'll be *more,* such a great mass of feeling I don't know how I'll cram it into my heart."

"We should probably wait to begin living together," he said reluctantly.

"Yes." She tried to be sensible. "Not—not too long. But I couldn't afford it just now, anyway. I think I need to open a bank account, and start putting money in it. I'm so cross with myself for not having saved anything!"

"I need another account, too, one I can't draw on. I always deposit my money straightaway in the bank, good as gold, and then a week later it's gone on bills and notes of hand. Might we make a pact, and go to the bank together?"

"I think that's the most romantic thing anyone's ever said to me."

"Yet." His blue eyes sparkled. "Give me time."

"I will," she promised.

Author's Note

Thank you for reading *All or Nothing*! I hope you enjoyed Simon and Maggie's story.

Would you like to know when my next book is available? Sign up for my newsletter at roselerner.com, or follow me on twitter at @roselerner or tumblr at http://roselerner.tumblr.com/.

Reviews help other readers find books. I appreciate all reviews, positive and negative.

Visit my website, roselerner.com, for free short stories and DVD extras like deleted scenes and historical research.

Turn the page to learn more about my other Regency romances.

True Pretenses

ROSE LERNER

...rich and memorable Regency romance...
—*Publishers Weekly* on *Sweet Disorder*

*N*ever steal a heart unless you can afford to lose your own.

Through sheer force of will, Ash Cohen raised himself and his younger brother from the London slums to become the best of confidence men. He's heartbroken to learn Rafe wants out of the life, but determined to grant his brother his wish.

It seems simple: find a lonely, wealthy woman. If he can get her to fall in love with Rafe, his brother will be set. There's just one problem—Ash can't take his eyes off her.

Heiress Lydia Reeve is immediately drawn to the kind, unassuming stranger who asks to tour her family's portrait gallery. And if she married, she could use the money from her dowry for her philanthropic schemes. The attraction seems mutual and oh so serendipitous—until she realizes Ash is determined to matchmake for his younger brother.

When Lydia's passionate kiss puts Rafe's future at risk, Ash is forced to reveal a terrible family secret. Rafe disappears, and Lydia asks Ash to marry her instead. Leaving Ash to wonder—did he choose the perfect woman for his brother, or for himself?

Warning: Contains secrets and pies.

Chapter One

B elow them in the darkness, a clock chimed half past two. "Just once, I'd like to leave somewhere in daylight," Rafe grumbled under his breath as they crept down the stairs. "Wearing my boots. I'd like to take my trunk with me too."

"Shh." Their trunk and its contents were worth twenty pounds. If Ash Cohen could have brought them away safely, he would have, but they meant exactly that to him—twenty pounds. The only thing he had that he couldn't leave behind was two feet in front of him, sulking.

His brother knew perfectly well that they left places in daylight with their trunks all the time. Only certain jobs—like this one—required sneaking off in the dead of night. But Rafe was always at his worst just after a successful swindle.

Ash supposed it was natural to feel empty and frustrated when an enterprise you'd spent weeks or months on was abruptly over. Ash himself would feel giddy, if his brother didn't insist on ruining his mood. Now instead of fizzing like a celebratory mug of ale, his chest cavity filled with—butterflies was too pretty a name for them. Moths, maybe, dirty-looking gray-and-white ones, swarming about and clinging to his innards.

At least Rafe didn't let pique spoil his concentration. He stepped unerringly around the squeaking, creaking places they'd scouted in the staircase, eased open the door on hinges they'd oiled, and shoved his feet silently into his boots. Ash did the same and followed his brother out into the night.

Rafe had never been able to hold a grudge for longer than ten miles, if Ash resisted the urge to cozen him. Today, it was nine and a half (calculated with their average speed of walking and Ash's watch) before he gave Ash a sidelong, apologetic smile and said, "I could eat a whole side of beef right now."

Ash relaxed. He wished he could be less sensitive to Rafe's moods, but it had been this way for twenty-five years now and showed no signs of changing. When baby Rafe had smiled and waved chubby little arms in his direction, nine-year-old Ash had felt special, important, as if he could vanquish lions. Before Rafe, he'd been nothing, one of an army of little street thieves. Ash smiled back and gave his brother a shove. "I've no doubt you could. Giant."

Rafe laid a large hand atop Ash's head. "Midget." Actually, Ash was of average height, and greater than average breadth. But Rafe towered over him, and that was Ash's greatest pride and accomplishment: one look, and you knew he'd always had enough to eat.

And people did look. Heads turned when Rafe walked into a room, huge and golden. Dark, sturdy Ash looked like an ox or a draft horse, his brute strength meant to carry others' burdens. Rafe was a thoroughbred. Maybe if Ash hadn't shared so many dinners with his little brother, he'd be a giant himself, but he had no regrets.

Another five miles and they were in complete charity with one another, and probably safe enough from pursuit to buy something to eat at a crowded inn. Rafe, more memorable, waited outside with his hat low over his face while Ash bought pasties and ale to be consumed a little way down the road.

Once the food was gone, however, Rafe's good spirits went with it. When he began worrying a worn handkerchief between his hands, Ash knew something was very wrong.

The scrap of fabric was all Ash had managed to keep when his mother died. Since he couldn't split his memories with his brother, Ash had given him the handkerchief as soon as Rafe was old enough to safeguard it from boys wanting to steal and sell it. He carried it always but almost never took it out.

"I'm sick of swindling," he said at last, with a heavy finality that Ash didn't like.

"You say that after every job. You'll be right as rain when we've found another flat. We always get on best when we're working."

"I'm sick of flats. I'm sick of a profession that hurts people. I want to be able to point to something I've done at the end of the day, something *good*."

Ash patted his pocket. "Two hundred pounds is a damn good thing, if you ask me."

Rafe frowned. "Other men give something back for money. They leave something behind them. We only take. I liked Mrs. Noakes."

"I liked her too," Ash said, stung. He liked everybody. That was why he was so good at his job. You couldn't swindle a person you couldn't get on with. "And she can afford to lose two hundred pounds."

Rafe turned his head away. "It isn't the money. Think of how she'll feel."

"Think of how we'd feel if we starved," Ash snapped. "We have to take care of ourselves—"

"—because no one will do it for us, I know." Rafe rarely raised his voice when he was angry. Most of the time, when he was trying to express an emotion other than happiness, he slowed down. It only meant he was struggling to find words, but in his deep voice, it gave every word a weight and echo, like a church bell tolling. Ash hated it. "I just want to make someone happy for a change."

You make me *happy.* The words stuck in Ash's throat. They really meant, *Don't I count?* They were weak and childish, and he knew the answer was no, anyway. He had brought Rafe up to take him for granted, to believe him strong and capable and impervious to the world's blows. He had wanted his brother to feel safe, as he himself never had. Fear, anxiety, illness, sadness—he'd protected Rafe with fierce care from them all. It seemed bitterly unfair that this was his reward.

"I don't enjoy the work anymore," Rafe said. "I'm sorry. I've tried and tried, but I find myself wishing the lies were true. That we were really shipwrecked Americans, or speculators who'd found copper on Mrs. Noakes's land, or anything other than thieves."

"You can't get—"

"—too fond of your own lies, I *know*. But haven't you ever, Ash?"

The dirty little moths settled back into his stomach and chest and clung. He had exactly one secret he'd never told Rafe.

Sometimes he forgot about it for days on end, and when he remembered, it was worse than stepping out of a warm shop into a snowstorm.

"Once." The word scraped his throat like a dull razor.

Rafe waited, but didn't press him. Ash wished he would. He wished Rafe would make him tell, because by now it was obvious he'd never find the courage otherwise. "Then you know what it's like," Rafe said finally. "I want to leave."

Everything stopped. The birds singing in the bare branches, the sun rising in the sky, Ash's heart beating in his chest—they all went silent and still. "Leave?"

Rafe held his gaze, earnest and sorrowful. It was the look he gave flats when he told them their money was gone, there'd been a ship lost at sea, a horse gone lame in the first lap, a bank failure. That was what made Rafe such a brilliant swindler: he had an honest face. Ash wanted to put his fist in it. "You can keep most of the money," Rafe offered. "I've thought about it. I could join the army—"

The money? Rafe thought he cared about the *money*? "You'll join the army? Even you can't be that stupid. Starve and fight and die for what? For England? What did England ever do for you? Men slice into their own legs with an ax to get *out* of the army!"

"Or I'll go to Canada. I've got to leave, Ash." He said it so slow and heavy it was like a judge pronouncing sentence. "I've done everything with you. Always. I don't know how to stop, without *stopping*. I won't be able to stick to it if you're there to talk me round. We both know it."

Resentment seared Ash's throat, sticky and hot as pitch. That was gammon. Rafe was the easygoingest man in the world right up until he dug in his heels, and then there was no moving him.

Rafe was going to leave, and Ash would be alone.

Instinctively, he bought himself time. "Well, if that's how you feel, I won't try to change your mind."

"Thank you for understanding. I didn't think you'd—you're the best of brothers." Rafe put an arm around his shoulder, his face glowing with...*relief*, Ash thought. Relief that Ash hadn't made an unpleasant scene. In spite of himself, Ash's stupid heart eased a little, that he'd made Rafe happy. "Thank you for everything. I'll—I'll miss you. I'll write you horribly misspelled letters, if you can think of a safe place to send them."

Mrs. Noakes had been a nice woman. Ash had liked her. But she'd grown up with a family, a home and plenty of food and clothes. She'd always have those things, two hundred pounds or no.

The world had given him and Rafe nothing, and they'd proved they didn't need it. Ash looked around at the muddy little clump of trees they stood in. The morning was cold and their breath misted in the air, but they were alive and well, with food in their bellies, good coats on their backs and good boots on their feet. The two of them against the world, and Ash would put his money on them every time. This little slice of England was all he'd ever wanted.

All Rafe wanted was to be somewhere else. Anywhere else. Now that Rafe had said it aloud, had given it shape, it made sense in a way Ash's idyllic picture of Two Wandering Jews never had. Rafe's depression between jobs was real, and his cheerfulness during a swindle was a brief intoxication. Ash had seen it too many times—dull-eyed, hopeless men who only found a spark of life when they could forget everything but the roll of the dice, the turn of the card, the pounding of the horses' hooves. He should have recognized it in his brother.

When Rafe had been hungry, Ash had found him food. When Rafe had been cold, Ash had got him clothes. When Rafe had been sick, Ash had brought him a doctor. He'd begged, borrowed, bargained, whored and stolen to do it— stolen every way he knew, and then made up a few new ones. He'd made it look easy, so Rafe would never feel how close they were to starving, freezing, dying of fever in a gutter somewhere and being dumped in paupers' graves.

Who would he even be, without Rafe? What right did Ash have to expect more than he'd already got?

What good did it do to be so angry, when he couldn't make Rafe want to stay anyway? It was twenty-five years too late for any sleight of hand. Rafe knew exactly what life with Ash was like, and he'd decided he didn't want it.

If Rafe wanted a new life, a respectable life, Ash would find a way to steal that for him too—one with no cannonballs or long sea journeys in it, either. And then, to keep himself from changing his mind, he'd do something he'd never done before. He'd give back something he'd stolen.

He'd tell Rafe everything.

Read the rest of Chapter One and buy the book at
roselerner.com/bookshelf/truepretenses

This novella was originally published in the anthology

Gambled Away

*G*et revenge. Pay a debt. Save a soul. Lose your heart.

Spanning centuries and continents, five brand-new novellas from beloved historical romance authors tell the stories of men and women who find themselves wagered in a game of chance and are forced to play for the highest stakes of all: love.

"Gideon and the Den of Thieves" by Joanna Bourne

London, 1793 – Soldier of fortune Gideon Gage has come home from halfway around the world, fully prepared to face down a ruthless gang to save his sister. But there's one member of the gang he could never have been prepared for: fascinating Aimée, driven from her own home by the French Revolution and desperately in need of his help.

"Raising The Stakes" by Isabel Cooper

California, 1938 — When the flute she won in last night's poker game unexpectedly summons an elven warrior bound to her service, two-bit con artist Sam takes quick advantage. With Talathan's fairy powers at her command, her shakedown of a crooked preacher is a sure thing...but would she rather take a gamble on love?

"All or Nothing" by Rose Lerner

England, 1819 – Architect Simon Radcliffe-Gould needs someone to pose as his mistress so he can actually get some work done at a scandalous house party. Irrepressible gambling den hostess Maggie da Silva would rather *be* his mistress, but she'll take what she can get…

"The Liar's Dice" by Jeannie Lin

Tang Dynasty China, 849 A.D. — Lady Bai's first taste of freedom brings her face to face with murder. A dangerous and enigmatic stranger becomes her closest ally as she investigates the crime, but can she trust her heart or her instincts when everyone is playing a game of liar's dice?

"Redeemed" by Molly O'Keefe

Denver, 1868 — After agonizing years in the Civil War's surgical tents, Union doctor James Madison has nothing left to lose. But when beautiful, tortured Helen Winters is the prize in a high-stakes game of poker, he goes all in to save her—and maybe his own soul.

Visit the other authors' websites to learn more about their stories.

Made in the USA
Monee, IL
27 August 2021